SPITE CLUB

MASON BROTHERS, BOOK 1

JULIE KRISS

ONE

Evie

It started with a phone call at one o'clock in the morning.

I'd put my pillow over my head to block out my roommate's music, and I pulled my head out when I heard the ringtone, my hair falling over my eyes as I reached for my phone. I didn't recognize the number. "Hello?"

A strange man's voice on the other end said, "Evie Bates?"

"Yes?" I croaked, half into my pillow in my dark bedroom.

"Is your boyfriend a guy named Josh Brantwell?"

"Yes." I sat bolt upright, shoving my hair back. "Oh my God, is he okay?"

"Not for long."

The man's voice was rough, as if he'd been shouting over a bar band all night, and I could hear the faint sounds of street noise in the background. I had never heard that voice before, and for a second I got a strange chill down my spine, like a premonition of doom.

"What?" I said. "What are you talking about?"

There was a pause. Then the man's voice came again, dark and cold. "Look, Evie Bates, I realize this is probably bad news, but I'm about to go beat your boyfriend to a pulp."

For a second, the words didn't compute. "Who is this?" I nearly shouted, standing up in the dark in my old pajama top.

"It's going to be bloody. I just thought I should warn you first."

"Is this a joke?" It didn't sound like a joke. It sounded like someone was about to beat up Josh. Was he being mugged? No, muggers didn't phone their victims' girlfriends first. And Josh couldn't get mugged unless he was out on the street somewhere, when I knew exactly where he was. He was—

"No joke," the strange man said. "My girlfriend is at Josh Brantwell's place right now. And I'm about to go mess him up."

That stopped me. It made no sense. "There's no girl at Josh's place," I said stupidly. "He's there alone."

"You sure about that?" the man said. "Because I followed my girlfriend tonight. And she came here." He rhymed off an address that made my stomach drop to the floor. "Resident is one Josh Brantwell."

"What is she doing there?" I said.

"Fucking him, I presume," the man said bluntly. "I'm pretty pissed off about it, I have to say. I'm about to go in there and give him a beating. But I looked him up first, and I saw that he has a girlfriend. So hey, Evie Bates, your asshole of a boyfriend is cheating on you. I thought you should know."

"I—" I couldn't think, couldn't speak. Josh? "I—"

"Well?" the man said.

"I have no idea what you're talking about."

"Yeah," the man said. "I thought so. Bring bandages, a towel, maybe a mop." Then he hung up.

For a second I stared at the wall of my bedroom, my mouth open.

Then I grabbed my clothes.

THERE WAS no way Josh was cheating on me. Simply no way. There had to be a mistake somewhere.

We'd been dating for four months. I met him at the bank where we were both tellers. He was dark-haired, clean-cut, good-looking, and when he asked me out I said yes. Of course I did. Josh was the Yeti of boyfriends: straight, single, sober, no baggage. I was twenty-five, and I was *supposed* to have a boyfriend like that. It was flattering that he'd picked me, when the other single women at work were circling him like sharks. I hadn't asked a lot of questions—I'd just gone on the date.

And it was going well. We got along. We liked the same TV shows. The sex was normal and semi-regular. I'd met his family, and he'd met my mother, who had pulled me aside and told me in a low voice that she could *see a future for me with a young man like that*. Finally, finally, I was putting in place everything I needed: a good job, a nice boyfriend, a regular life, my mother's approval. It was finally happening.

The call could be a fake. Maybe this guy—I had no idea who he was—was just crazy. Maybe he was a serial killer, trying to lure me to my death. But I thought about the voice I'd heard on the phone, rough and a little dangerous, and I felt that chill again. The stranger hadn't sounded like a serial killer. He'd sounded honest and very, very pissed off.

Still, I told myself there was a mistake somewhere. The stranger's cheating girlfriend had gone to a different address, not Josh's. Or something. Because Josh was definitely, definitely not cheating.

Right?

I gripped the wheel and pulled up to Josh's condo complex

and thought about signs. Were there signs when a guy was cheating? What were they supposed to be? We didn't have sex often, but then we never had. That was what happened when you were in a regular relationship, I'd told myself calmly. That was real life. No one went around having sex all the time, anyway. You did it on a schedule, when you were free and you were both in the mood. Had we been having sex even less than usual? When was the last time? I stared at the door of his building and thought back. Saturday night? No, he'd gone out with his friends. It must have been before that.

How else was I supposed to know he was cheating? We didn't fight. He got a lot of attention from female coworkers and customers at work, but he didn't make a big deal about that. He didn't act furtive, and I hadn't caught him lying. In fact, I'd been starting to think about having the Big Conversation with him. The one about Us and Our Future and Maybe Moving In. I had a schedule. I *needed* a schedule. Without a schedule, I would mess everything up. I was determined not to mess up this time. I was determined to make it work.

Bring bandages, a towel, maybe a mop.

I got that chill of premonition again.

No. Just no. I was going to handle this. And everything would be fine.

It was raining, a warm June rain. We'd just come off of a cold, shitty Michigan winter, and even the rain was welcome after the months of snow. I got out of the car and walked up Josh's driveway, letting myself get wet. Josh lived in a complex of townhouse condos, attached in a long line like one of those cutout crafts you did in public school. The complex was brand new. It was his first place, bought with his nice bank salary. In every way, my boyfriend was on the way up.

There was a second car in the driveway, parked behind Josh's treasured Mustang. A pretty little car, as red as lipstick. And beyond that, parked on the street, was another black car I didn't recognize, inky in the darkness.

There was no one around. This was a neighborhood of nice young professionals, tidy and brand new, unlike the rest of Millwood, Michigan. This wasn't where the drunks and the teenagers and the pot dealers hung out. This was where people had jobs they had to get up for in the morning, and they all went to bed at ten.

There were lights on in Josh's place. An upstairs light, and a light downstairs in the living room. More ominously, the front door was open. Just a little—it was a few inches ajar—but it was open. And something was going on inside. A man was bellowing. A woman was shouting. There was a thump, a crash of something breaking.

Oh, shit.

I ran the rest of the way up the driveway. A neighboring door opened, and a woman of about thirty-five stepped on to her porch, giving me a total bitch face that could turn you into stone from twenty feet away. "I'm about to call the cops!" she shouted at me. "See if I don't! I can hear them straight through the connecting wall!"

"Don't do it!" I shouted back. I ran past her to Josh's doorway.

Inside, the living room was carnage. Josh's nice Ikea coffee table was overturned, and one of the brand-new blinds had been ripped from the living room window—it hung crazily, making the whole room look like it was on an angle.

Josh was lying on the floor, curled up in pain, his hands over his face. Blood seeped through his fingers. He was wearing nothing but a pair of tighty whities, his gym-toned body on display. Standing next to him, shouting *Stop*, was a woman with long, dark curly hair. She was gorgeous and sexy, and she was wearing a t-shirt I recognized as Josh's, and obviously nothing else. I could literally see her bare ass.

That answered the cheating question, then.

Something inside me snapped, and I went numb. I stopped seeing Josh's nice living room, where we'd watched TV and made out with his hand down my pants. I stopped seeing the nice furniture, some of which I'd helped him pick out. I stopped seeing his nice body, that I'd had sex with on a nice regular schedule for four nice months. I stopped seeing anything at all except that woman's bare ass, perfectly round and much smaller than mine, beneath the hem of my boyfriend's T-shirt.

Was that feeling heartbreak? I didn't know. Embarrassment? Pain? Maybe it was just the feeling of all of your life's plans flushing down the toilet in a single second.

Then I noticed the man.

Standing over Josh, looking down at him, was a guy I didn't know. He was wearing beat-up jeans, motorcycle boots—one of which was untied—and a gray T-shirt so worn that the hem had come unstitched. A brown leather jacket lay discarded on the floor at his feet. His hands were curled into fists, his arms flexed. They were impressive arms, sleek with muscle. In fact, all of him was impressive—his shoulders, his back through the thin shirt, his narrow waist. He had tousled brown hair, a scruff of stubble, a face that knocked me back. My first thought was *Jesus, he's good-looking.* Everyone in this little scene was good-looking except, maybe, me. And they were all so focused that not a single one of them had noticed me.

"Hey," I said.

Everyone turned and looked at me. It was like a crazy tableau, and for a second it hurt so sickeningly much that I felt like laughing. *Evie Finds Boyfriend With Pants Down.* I was breathless with pain, but I was also a little detached. *Is this really happening? Why can't I feel anything? What's wrong with me?*

Josh dropped his hands from his face, and I could see blood dripping from his nose. "*Evie!*" he said, in a tone of such pure horror it was almost comical. I felt like laughing again. Or maybe screaming.

The bare-assed woman took her turn. "Oh, my God!" she cried, dropping to her knees. "Josh!" She touched him gingerly, getting close to but not quite touching any blood. She looked up at the man above her. "Stop hitting him, Nick, you asshole!"

But Nick, the asshole, wasn't even looking at her. He was looking at me.

He was still poised in his fight stance, his fists curled, but instead of looking angry or threatening, he looked... distracted. His gaze took me in, up and down, and then it rested on my face, his eyes catching mine, as if he was trying to figure something out.

I was wearing a green T-shirt and denim overalls. Okay, fine, overalls aren't exactly fashionable, but they were the first things I pulled off the floor. The overalls, plus the gray cardigan I'd put on, hid the fact that I wore no bra, so that was a win. May in Michigan, especially in the middle of the night, is not exactly warm, and my nipples were showing the fact behind the overalls. I had flip-flops on my feet—my toes were wet and freezing—and my shoulder-length hair was a mess, my face devoid of makeup and probably creased with sleep. I wasn't exactly Giselle, but at least my ass was covered.

"Evie," Josh said from the floor. "I can explain."

"Nick, he's bleeding!" the beautiful woman shrieked. "Should we call an ambulance? What do we do?"

"No ambulance!" Josh replied. He rolled over and groaned, cupping his bleeding nose. The only person who didn't say anything was Nick, who was still looking at me.

Despite the craziness of the scene, and my hurt, and the fact that my boyfriend had—it seemed likely—recently put his dick into the bare-assed girl, I was calm. *Be polite*, my mother had always taught me. *No one likes a girl who makes a fuss.* That's who I was now. I was the polite girl, after years of failure at it. I ran a hand through my hair, thinking maybe I *should* make a fuss in this situation—but then again, Josh and the gorgeous woman were making enough of a fuss for everyone.

I met Nick's gaze without flinching. I couldn't read his expression.

"The neighbors are about to call the cops," I told him in my oddly normal voice.

He blinked once—his eyelashes were ridiculously dark—and looked down at Josh, who was still moaning. I watched him uncurl his fists. He toed Josh with his boot, nudging him in the ribs as the woman poked at him, still not getting bloody. "Hey," he said, the voice I recognized from the phone call. "Shut up."

The woman wasn't done. "You asshole!" she shouted at Nick again.

Nick actually sighed. "You shut up, too, Gina," he said. She went quiet, still glaring.

I should be screaming, or crying maybe. I should be losing my shit. Instead, I watched as Nick bent and picked up his brown leather jacket, shrugged it on. He scrubbed a hand over his face. His knuckles were red—he'd given Josh a hell of a hit. There was a second of furious satisfaction at that, and then I pushed it down again. That wasn't me.

Ignoring the two on the floor, Nick walked toward me, his untied boot clomping loudly. I felt a jolt of alarm low in my belly. I'd met bad boys in my life—even done things I shouldn't with a few of them, back when I was Old Evie—but I'd never seen one like this. This Nick guy owned a room without even trying. He probably wrecked things without even trying, too. Lives. Women. Virginities. Reputations. He was that kind of guy.

Still, I assumed that with his ass-kicking finished he would leave, and Old Evie felt a pang over it. I didn't know who Nick was, but he was very fucking cool, and I envied him that. Old

Evie would have followed a guy like this like a lapdog. "Thanks for the phone call," I said to him.

He stopped, looking at me again in that way he had, like he was figuring something out. "Yeah?"

"I mean it." I did. If he hadn't called me, I would have continued getting cheated on, not knowing about it. It wasn't his fault. "It takes guts to be the bearer of bad news."

Nick considered that, his gorgeous gray eyes looking me over. "Are you pissed off, Evie Bates?" he asked in his bar-band growl.

It was a strange question, but somehow it fit the strange, surreal night I was having. I looked past him at Josh and naked girl, who were watching us. Josh had sat up, and I could see his nicely styled hair, his washboard stomach. He'd had sex with me a week ago, on my bed in my apartment. I remembered now.

Old Evie would have screamed at Josh. New Evie didn't make a fuss.

But maybe both Evies were angry.

I nodded, answering Nick's question. "Yeah. I think I'm pissed off."

"Yeah?" Nick said. "Okay, then. You hungry?"

Another weird question, but suddenly I was. I really fucking was. It was like he was hypnotizing me. I shouldn't do this, not even a little. I should tell him to take a hike.

I should go home and get back in bed and pull up the covers and handle this like an adult. I should get some sleep so I'd be ready for work in a few hours. I should be rational and work through it and partake in self-care and do whatever you were supposed to do when your boyfriend cheated on you. I should work on getting past this and healing. I should get through this and come out better and stronger than before. Giving in to base instincts was not going to help with any of that.

I looked at Nick. It was two in the morning. I was pissed. And he was ridiculously hot.

Bad idea, Evie.

Shut up, Old Evie said.

"I'm starving," I told Nick.

He nodded back. It was like he understood everything.

"Me too," he said. "Let's go."

TWO

Evie

His full name, it turned out, was Nick Mason. Half an hour later we sat in an all-night diner, ordering food from the pasty waitress. Millwood was a trucker's town, a factory worker's town—or it had been until the gentrifying started—and all-night places weren't all that rare here. Even now, a trucker sat at a table nursing a cup of coffee, and another one wolfed down a piece of pie before hitting the road again. Outside, the rain had turned into wet mist that beaded in your hair and on your clothes without really turning into rain again.

The waitress didn't hand us any menus, so I asked her, "What is the kitchen making right now?"

She shrugged. "Grilled cheese sandwich. Three bucks."

My stomach growled so loud we all heard it.

"Done," Nick said, and the waitress walked away.

I stared at the man across the booth from me. In keeping with the surreal nature of tonight, he was good-looking even in the fluorescent light of a diner at two a.m. Gray eyes with short dark lashes, high cheekbones, a sculpted mouth. Life was very fucking unfair. He wasn't even trying to look that good. His hair was damp and mussed, his stubble an exact shade of hangover, and there was a hole just below the collar of his T-shirt. He looked like a model, if a model had rolled off the back of a truck or woken up in the drunk tank—or both. He stuck the straw in his ice water in the corner of his mouth and watched me back.

"Well, that was a scene," I commented.

"Sorry," he said. "I had to do it."

I traced my finger down the side of my water glass. "How did you find me?" I asked. "I mean, you said how you found Josh. But how did you find me?"

"The internet." He put down his water. "It wasn't advanced detective work. I'm not that smart."

I nodded. I was probably on Josh's Facebook page, from the times he'd posted when we went out for dinner or with friends. Which we would never do again. "I'm sort of in shock," I said. "I didn't, um. I didn't know. At all."

"No?" Nick said. "I did. That is, I knew she was fucking someone. I didn't know who."

Fucking someone. So much coarser than *cheating,* but it meant the same thing. "Things were going so well," I said. It hit me again, that punch in the gut of hurt. "I *thought* they were. But I guess not." I closed my eyes as yet another detail occurred to me. "I have to work at the bank with him. Oh my god, I'm so humiliated."

"You love him?" Nick asked.

I opened my eyes again and looked at him. "What? I don't—I mean, I hadn't really... It wasn't..." Love? Had I even asked myself that? And why was I talking about it with this guy? "Do you always ask personal questions?"

"Just wondering if you're going to cry, that's all. If you do, I might bail." He put down his water glass. "You want to talk about the weather right now, Evie?" he said. "For real?"

Intense. That was what he was. Intense. No one who worked at the bank—and I mean no one—was intense. Even Old Evie, in her wild days, hadn't met a guy like this. If you were going to spill your guts to someone, it may as well be a gorgeous stranger in the middle of the night. But I didn't say any more. Instead I said, "How long has it been going on?"

"A week? Two?" Nick picked up his spoon and spun it deftly over his fingers, then put it down again. "I could tell something was up. Jesus Christ, my girlfriend fucked a bank guy." He rolled his eyes.

"Hey—I dated him," I said, stung. "And I'm a bank... person. What does Miss Bare-Assed Gina do?"

"She's a massage therapist."

I thought of her long, slim legs, given to her by God and genetics. "She's pretty," I said self-pityingly.

"Not anymore," Nick replied.

"She's better-looking than me," I said while our waitress put down our sandwiches. "Thinner. Obviously. I mean, Josh is better-looking than me. Everyone always wondered how I got such a good-looking guy. They all wondered what he was doing with me. I should have known."

Nick took a bite of his sandwich. "You done?" he asked.

I looked down at the gooey cheese on my plate. Fuck, it looked delicious. I shouldn't eat it. "Done what?"

"Pissing on yourself," he said. "Whining."

I looked up and froze, staring at him. "Excuse me?"

"You heard me," he said. "You want to feel better, you should fuck someone. It'll do a better job than wasting time running yourself down like that."

For a second I couldn't say anything. Then I found my voice. "Did you just say I should fuck someone?"

"You heard me. You should," he said. "Hard. Get someone to fuck you until you can't stand up." His gaze went up and down me again, seeming to see through my clothes. "I'm gonna guess Bank Boy never fucked you like that."

No. Josh had never fucked me like that. However Nick meant when he looked at me just that way... No. Another shiver happened low in my belly.

I had to be rational here. And I didn't even *know* this guy.

"I can't—" I stuttered. "I can't believe you just said that. You're an asshole."

"That right there." He pointed at me, at my face. He wore two bracelets on his wrist, a leather one and a woven one that looked old and worn. Something significant. I wondered what it was. "That expression. That's the one you didn't have when you saw your boyfriend fucking another woman. I bet Bank Boy never saw that expression at all."

I had no idea what my expression was, but I had to guess furious. Because that was how I suddenly felt. Fuck him and his stupid insights, anyway. "Fine," I said, trying to piss him off in return. "I should just fuck someone. Are you volunteering?"

For a second, he actually considered it, his gaze taking me in, up and down. My overalls and sweater, my messy hair. My stomach went into freefall. Why had I said that? Because he was hot, and I'd assumed it wouldn't happen? Or because I assumed it would? If he said no, or if he said yes—either was equally terrifying.

But Nick shook his head. "You're not the kind of woman I fuck," he said.

Now I was both offended and relieved at the same time. "Why not?" I asked.

"You're nice. I'm too dirty for you."

No one likes a girl who makes a fuss, my mother said in my head. Gina wasn't *nice*. Gina was sexy. Dirty, maybe. Unlike me. Unlike the way I was now.

There were reasons I was like this. Being sexy and dirty, being that girl—it led nowhere. It was pointless. Worse, it led to pain and disappointment. No, even for Nick Mason and his stupid-gorgeous face and his stupid-hot body, I wasn't going down that road ever again.

But suddenly I was purely, deeply enraged. I wanted to stand up, flip the table through the plate glass window, and scream that *I was not nice.*

I didn't do that, of course. I sat with my hands gripping the table edge so hard my knuckles were white. If Nick noticed, he didn't let on. "Well, you're not my type either," I snapped. "I like guys with a little politeness and self-respect. I also like guys who do laundry every once in a while."

He put a hand over his heart. "You're hurting me," he said. "What are you, seventy? You look twenty-five at most. Loosen up, have some orgasms. You're missing out."

"You don't know what I'm missing."

"Yeah, redhead, I kind of do."

Fuck. He was so calm. And he had sexy fucking arms. Sexy everything. I kept my voice snappish to keep my distance. "So, Dr. Freud, I should have orgasms, according to you. Is that right? But not with you."

"Definitely not with me."

"What is the matter with you?" I said, so loud the half-asleep waitress behind the front counter nearly woke all the way up.

"What's the matter with me is that I'm an asshole," Nick said. "We've established that. What's the matter with you?"

"What's the matter with me is that I wasted four months!" I said. "*Four months* on that jerk! Being *nice!* He was supposed to be the one! We were supposed to make *plans!* And he went off and banged some massage therapist with no pants, and you think I should just—should just—"

"Fuck someone," Nick supplied.

"Is that what *you're* going to do?" Oh, God. Suddenly, I had a vision: Nick Mason, naked, in bed. I looked at his perfect mouth, and the dip between his collarbones, which I could see past the neck of his T-shirt, and it was so easy to picture. All that taut, muscled skin. It was all mixed up with his muscles and his reddened knuckles and the gravel of his voice, and suddenly my girl parts woke up. I mean *woke up*. I didn't even like him, and he'd just insulted me. It was exciting and horrifying at the same time.

"I might fuck someone," he answered me, oblivious. "I'm still considering. I punched Bank Boy, and that felt pretty good. It's you who has the anger problem."

That startled me out of my lust. "I do not have an anger problem."

"You do," he corrected me patiently. "Your problem is that you don't have enough of it. You need to get good and mad."

"I am already good and mad," I argued back. "At you."

"Then take it out on me," Nick said, immune to my insults. "I'm at a boxing gym every day at five." He told me an address that I recognized in a not-so-nice part of town. "Come meet me if you want to work up a sweat."

My reply was immediate. A boxing gym? With Nick Mason? "No way."

He licked cheese from his thumb, pulled some bills from his wallet, and stood up. "Whatever. See you later, redhead." Then he turned and walked for the door.

I stared after him, stunned. And I couldn't help it. I watched his ass as he walked.

It was amazing.

I stared for a long time after he was gone, still picturing it.
Then I ate my damned sandwich.

THREE

Nick

A redhead in overalls. *Overalls.* What the hell?

She wasn't my type of woman at all. I didn't really *have* a type, except maybe "willing to put up with my shit" and "too self-involved to ask questions." Evie Bates was neither. I shouldn't have paid any attention to her. I should have just punched Bank Boy, dumped Gina, and moved on.

But I hadn't. Oh, I'd punched him all right—Gina and I may not have been Romeo and Juliet, but no guy can stay calm at the idea of his girlfriend taking another guy's dick. And as for dumping her, I suppose I'd made it pretty clear that Gina and I were done.

But then Evie Bates had walked in.

She had brown-reddish hair, brown eyes, clear skin, and a nice, rounded body. She didn't look like a lingerie model or a party girl, but she didn't have to. She was very fucking hot in a way I could appreciate, even with Gina's bare, cheating ass on display.

But I was right when I said she was nice. It came off her like a smell—a nice smell, but still a smell. She was a nice girl, with a nice boyfriend, who was obviously keeping her chin up through the shock and hurt when she caught him fucking someone else. That look on her face when she came through the door made me want to punch Bank Boy all over again.

And again, in the diner, her feelings had been *right there.* She'd practically put them on the table between us. Feelings were not something I was familiar with. Feelings were not how I roll. Except anger. And when Evie stopped looking hurt and started getting angry, I decided to see if she would agree to come hit me.

So sue me, I was curious. But that's all it was. I wasn't about to mess around with a girl that nice.

It was four o'clock in the morning now, and as I let myself into my loft apartment I heard the unmistakable clicking of dog toenails on my hardwood floor. Gina's fucking dog. Her name was Scout, she was a Chihuahua, and Gina had given her to me because her landlord had implemented a no-pets policy. I didn't want a dog, but Gina had begged me. There was no one else to take the thing, and it would get put to sleep. So now Scout lived with me.

I opened the door, and she came running, her tiny body wiggling in excitement, her tongue lolling. She stood on her hind legs—she only came to my knee like that—and scrabbled her tiny paws, which I could barely feel through the cloth of my jeans. This meant she wanted to be let out.

"I can't believe this," I grumbled at her as I grabbed the leash from the hook, which made her nearly explode with excitement. "Gina cheats on me, and I'm stuck with her stupid dog." I looked Scout over as I clipped the leash to her pink collar. "Are you even a real dog, anyway? I'm not sure."

Scout took my insults happily, trying to lick my face before I could stand up again. I dodged her—I knew where she put that tongue. We went outside and she did her business, her happy as fuck, me shivering in the drizzle and tired now as the events of the night set in. A few early-shift people were setting off to work, giving me curious looks as I waited for my Chihuahua with her pink collar to finish peeing. I wished I had a sign saying *She's not my dog, I'm just stuck with her.*

I wasn't a dog person. I wasn't an anything person. I took Scout back upstairs, gave her some of her kibble, stripped down to nothing but a pair of sweatpants, and lay on my sofa, staring at the ceiling.

I had a loft apartment in downtown Millwood. It had been some kind of industrial building once upon a time, but it had been made over into artsy lofts that were right downtown and overly expensive. My neighbors were mostly lawyers and such.

I wasn't a lawyer. I wasn't anything. In fact, I was one hundred percent unemployed. And the loft was all mine, because of my trust fund. Sounds great, and it was, but my family was ten kinds of fucked up, plus my girlfriend had just banged a bank guy. Money buys a lot of things, but not everything.

It wasn't my usual thing, to follow my girlfriend around, hoping to catch her cheating. I wasn't a suspicious guy by nature, and as far as I'm concerned, when we're not together and we're not fucking, what a woman does with her time is her business. Just like what I do with my time is mine.

But I would have had to be a blind man not to see that Gina was screwing someone. Calling off dates, lying about where she was going, having her friends lie for her—she may as well have worn a neon sign. It's one thing to get dumped—*you won't let us get serious, you're too closed off, you have no feelings,* I've heard them all—and another to be cheated on behind your back. First it made me suspicious, and then it made me mad. And I got even madder when I saw the guy she'd cheated with.

Seriously? That guy? With his carefully crafted stubble and

his tighty whities? Maybe I'm not much of a boyfriend, but I have to be better than *that* guy. I don't call much and I don't tell the women I date anything important about myself, but at least I'm not high on myself and I know how to fuck.

Again, I saw the hurt cross Evie's face, clear as day. Like someone had punched her in the stomach. Bank Boy had done that—hurt her like that. And again, lying on my couch and staring at the ceiling, that still bothered me.

Shit.

I drifted off on the sofa, my mind wandering to pleasant daydreams of Evie's soft cherry lips on my dick, which was half-hard in my sweatpants because I'm an asshole. I woke up three hours later with a kink in my neck and Scout buried firmly in my armpit, curled tight into a ball and sound asleep. And damn it, I was still thinking about Evie Bates.

This wasn't over yet. I had a feeling.

But first, I had to go visiting.

FOUR

Evie

Josh called in sick to work the next day. I wanted to think it was because he was sorry, but deep down I knew it was because his face was probably bruised to a pulp, and he didn't want to show up. Well, that was too bad. Unless he wanted to take the whole week off, he was going to have to show up sometime.

But I had today free of him. I had Nick Mason to thank for that.

Hey, where's Josh? people said to me in the hallway at the bank branch I worked at in downtown Millwood. The central branch of this particular bank, in fact. The most important branch. The branch where the best people worked, because here they could get promoted.

These were nice people, well-dressed and pleasant, and they could recommend me when the next promotion came up. So I couldn't just tell everyone to please, please fuck off.

Sick, huh? You see him? He okay?

I'd always liked it before, that everyone knew Josh was my

boyfriend. It was a badge. A New Evie badge. Now it was like water torture, gritting my teeth and smiling at people, shrugging, shaking my head. *I don't know. I'm sure he's fine.* By lunchtime I felt like an overinflated balloon that might pop if you poked it.

I sat in my little bank teller cubicle and took customers one by one, while my stomach churned and I wondered what was wrong with me that Josh would cheat. Did I not pay attention to him? Did I do something wrong? Was a too boring, too fat? Then I hated myself for thinking like that. It was like someone had set a toxic thought chain off inside my head that wouldn't stop.

But I didn't make a fuss. I kept calm. I needed this job. I'd made a mess of high school and dropped out of college, and now, at twenty-five, I needed to do something with my life. Something that involved pencil skirts and low heels and regular paychecks. Something I could get promoted at. Something that made sense.

Josh had been part of that. I'd wanted—needed—someone stable, acceptable. Except either he'd been a very good liar, or I hadn't seen what I didn't want to see.

Okay, so my relationship had turned into a dumpster fire, but I would deal. Dumpster fires could be contained. I still needed the rest of my life to work.

By the end of the day, my jaw hurt like I'd had it in a vise, and the back of my neck was so tense it felt like glass. I had a throbbing headache and my feet hurt—but I'd made it. I was powering down the computer in my cubicle when one of my coworkers, Dar, came over, pulling on her coat. "Hey," she said. "A bunch of us are going for a drink. Want to come?"

I pretended to think it over, though today of all days I'd rather put my eye out. "I don't think so," I said. "I'm tired." Translation: I wanted to go home, put on my baggy pajamas, and curl up in bed, listening to my roommate Heather blare the Pet Shop Boys in her room. Heather's musical taste was stuck in the eighties, but except for the REO Speedwagon, I didn't really mind.

"Come on," Dar said, zipping her coat. "It'll be fun. Call up Josh. I bet he's not even sick. He'll probably come."

My headache throbbed harder. I picked up my own coat from the coat rack. "The thing is, Dar, Josh and I broke up."

Her nicely plucked eyebrows rose up to her hairline, but that was all. She blinked once. "Oh."

"Yeah, I'm really sorry, I—" I stopped and stared at her. "You're not shocked."

"Sure I am," she said, stepping forward and squeezing my shoulder. "I'm sorry, hon. Let's go drink."

"No, wait." I pulled back and looked at her expression again. Dar was thirty, with dark blond hair and great makeup. "You really don't look surprised."

"Well..." She squeezed my shoulder again, uncomfortable, and dropped her hand. "You two just didn't seem compatible, I guess."

"What does that mean?" I was feeling a dark, awful twinge of panic deep in my chest.

"Well, you know." Now she looked really uncomfortable and couldn't quite meet my eyes. "You're looking for something serious, and Josh wasn't quite ready to settle down."

There was a long, painful silence, as drawn out as a scream.

And it hit me. "Oh, my god," I said. "You knew."

Now she looked panicked. "I don't know what you mean."

"How could you possibly know?" I said. "I mean, how could everyone know except me? Did he wear a sign?"

"Honey, it isn't like that," Dar said. "It was just..." She trailed off.

"Just what?"

"They, um..." Dar looked like she wished she could sink into the floor. "They weren't very discreet."

Which meant everyone knew. Everyone.

I looked around. Margaret was packing up her purse. Adam

was locking the front doors. Gail, my manager, was locking her office and leaving.

It was Gail who gave it away. She caught my eye quickly as she turned to go—the first time she'd looked at me all day. Then she gave me a little apologetic wave and hurried away.

Everyone knew.

"You should go out with Dave in Client Management," Dar said. "He's divorced, and a single dad. He's super stable, dependable, and cute too. He was asking about you at the last Christmas party. I think he likes you."

I jerked on my coat and picked up my purse. "I think I'll just go home."

I hurried through the parking lot—it was raining again—and got into my car, slamming the door. I was breathing hard. How was this happening? And how had everyone at the bank known about Gina? Had she come into the bank or something? Was she a customer? I had no idea how they'd even met. *When* they'd met.

So hey, your asshole of a boyfriend is cheating on you, Evie Bates.

All of those nice people at work, and not one of them had cared enough to tell me. Even though he was a jerk, Nick, at least, had had the guts to say the truth.

It was infuriating.

Maybe you should fuck someone, his low growl of a voice said.

"Be quiet," I said out loud.

Get someone to fuck you until you can't stand up.

"Shut up," I said to the empty car. "I'm not fucking anyone. I'm going home to bed."

Come meet me if you want to work up a sweat.

And then: *You're not the kind of woman I fuck.*

Maybe he'd found someone else already. Some woman who looked like a Victoria's Secret model, loved anal and one-night stands, and had no baggage. *Dirty,* he'd said. That seemed like

Nick's kind of woman, instead of neurotic bank tellers who had quit Weight Watchers twice and sat alone ranting and raving in their cars.

Have some orgasms. You're missing out.

Those muscles. That ass. That mouth, that fuck-me voice. New Evie never got guys like that. God, I hated him.

I *should* have a guy like that. Hot, muscled, and dirty. A few hours of no-holds-barred fun for once, instead of it always being about who's acceptable, who's long term. Just... *fucking*. Like Nick had said.

Except not with Nick.

The phone rang, startling me out of my crazy thoughts. "Are you kidding me?" I said when I answered, because Josh didn't deserve *hello*.

"Evie." Josh's voice was slightly muffled, probably because his nose was swollen. "We have to talk."

"No," I said. "We really don't."

"I get that you're mad. What I did was wrong. Just don't say anything at work, okay?"

"People already know," I said. "In fact, people at work knew before I did."

Now he sounded panicked. "Who told? What did they say?"

For God's sake. Why did he sound so freaked about a secret that was already out? "Ask everyone yourself. Goodbye."

"Wait, Evie, wait! Just give me a minute. I fucked up, I know. But our relationship wasn't working. You know that."

That hurt. "It seemed like it was working to me. But then again, I guess I'm not very smart."

"Evie. You and I didn't have very much... spark."

This day, this awful day, blew past my limit at a hundred miles per hour. The words were out before I could stop them. "*I have plenty of fucking spark!*" I shouted into the phone, my voice bouncing off the close confines of the car.

There was a moment of stunned silence—from both of us.

"Okay," Josh said at last. "But I'm worried about you, because you left with that guy last night."

"Nick?" I said.

"Oh Christ, you know his name. Did you not *see* what he did to me? That guy is violent and crazy. He nearly broke my nose!"

"You slept with his girlfriend," I pointed out.

"It was assault!" Josh was worked up now. "First degree! I could have had a concussion or something! I could have called the cops! That guy is a complete fucking animal. Don't you know who he is?"

"Am I supposed to?" I asked. "Is he a rock star or something?" I could kind of see that, actually.

"No, he's not a rock star, for God's sake. He doesn't do anything at all."

"What does that mean?"

"It means he doesn't do anything. He has no job." This, in Josh's world, was a cardinal sin. "Gina told me all about him," he ranted on. "He's a spoiled rich kid. He lives off his trust fund. His own parents hate his guts. All he does is party—he does nothing but live it up. Stay away from him, Evie. He's completely irresponsible and he has no respect for anything. He's a loose cannon. He's not the kind of guy you want to date."

For a second, I almost said *How do you know what kind of guy I want to date?* Then I remembered that the kind of guy I wanted to date had been him. Until last night.

Strange. Nick hadn't given any indication he was rich. His clothes certainly hadn't given it away.

But I was sure Josh was right about this. If for no other reason than because Josh was so mad, and the only thing that could work him up like this was a guy who was cooler, better-looking, and richer—without working!—than he was.

"I thought Nick was hot," I said, just to make Josh angrier.

"All those muscles. And the way he punched you—definitely sexy."

"Stop it," Josh said. "I know what you're doing, Evie. You're trying to get back at me, and it's childish. I'm just trying to help you."

"*Help* me?"

"Nick Mason is scum. He'll take advantage of you. Of your hurt feelings. You're vulnerable right now."

"You have got to be kidding me," I said.

"Evie, come on, you're smarter than this. You'd never stoop to date a guy like him. He'll probably hit on you, because he's that kind of jerk. I'm telling you, don't do it."

Josh didn't know about Old Evie, because I'd never told him. Old Evie was my shameful secret, because Old Evie, in her day, had stooped pretty low. Josh, I realized now, would never have understood Old Evie. Never in a million years.

"You don't get a say in who I date," I told Josh. "Not anymore. Maybe I'd *like* Nick to come on to me. Maybe I'll say yes when he does." *If he does.* "At least he isn't a cheater, and he's hot."

"Evie, stop acting like a child."

"Fuck you, Josh. I have to go." I hung up.

Chew on that, Josh.

I'd implied something would happen between me and Nick, without saying anything outright. It would probably bug him for hours. It was petty, and I liked it. I was allowed to be fucking petty.

But the words kept going through my head as I drove home.

All he does is party.

He's completely irresponsible.

A loose cannon.

You'd never stoop to date a guy like him.

He was probably right. I'd met Nick, if only briefly, and all signs pointed to a guy who was lazy, irresponsible, and completely spoiled. Not to mention rude and insulting. The kind of guy I absolutely should have nothing to do with.

But it had made Josh so mad.

Josh had no idea, but he'd just made Nick Mason sound like the perfect man.

FIVE

Nick

My brother's house was in one of Millwood's suburbs, on a street of one-story bungalows dating from the seventies. Most of his neighbors were factory workers and secretaries, and like me, Andrew didn't fit in with his neighbors. But he had different reasons than I did.

I picked up two cups of coffee on my way and when I pressed the buzzer at his front door, I made sure to wave the cups in front of the security camera. There was barely a heartbeat before Andrew buzzed me in.

He was in his computer room, which used to be the living room, where some seventies family would watch TV. Now it was filled with expensive custom equipment and piled-up dishes. Andrew was at one of his keyboards, typing code, and he barely glanced up when I came in the room.

"You look like shit," he said, going back to his typing.

I put the coffees down on the edge of a messy, overcrowded desk. "I didn't realize it was a beauty contest."

"Good, because you'd fail."

"Tough crowd," I said. "I guess I'll just drink these two coffees by myself, then."

"Fuck you, Mason," Andrew said. "Give me one of those before I wheel over there and kick your ass."

Andrew was my older brother, and my only sibling. He was a programmer. He was also in a wheelchair, since he was in a car accident five years ago at age twenty-three. This was the reason he lived in an old bungalow—because there were no stairs. If you think this is some sad story about a guy in a wheelchair, think again.

"You really do look like ass," he said when I handed him his coffee. "What's going on?"

I sat down and swigged my coffee. Andrew was wearing sweatpants and a white t-shirt, four days' worth of beard on his jaw. He lived alone and didn't give much of a shit about his appearance. Kind of like me, except I had a Chihuahua and I could still walk.

Andrew was also the only person I talked to regularly, so I came out with it. "Gina screwed some other guy," I said. "I caught them together and punched him. Now we're over. Oh, and I'm stuck with her stupid dog."

Andrew lowered his coffee and his eyes went wide. "Oh shit." He paused. "You're stuck with her dog?"

I glared at him. "You are such an asshole."

"Okay, okay. I couldn't help it." His expression softened. "I'm sorry to hear that, man. That sucks."

We were quiet for a minute. This was our version of an emotional moment.

"At least you punched him," Andrew finally said. "Did he bleed?"

I flexed my sore knuckles. The anger rose up for a second,

pure and red and hot. I'd thought I was done with it, but I needed a session at the boxing gym. "Yeah, he bled."

Andrew swigged his coffee. His hair and eyes were darker than mine, his face thinner and more sharp because of what he'd been through, his body a little smaller, but otherwise it was like looking in a mirror. "I have to tell you, man, I didn't think it would work."

I looked at him, surprised. "You didn't meet her." I'd never brought Gina to meet Andrew—I'd never brought any woman, ever, to meet Andrew. I never even *told* women about him. When it came to Andrew, in my opinion you either earned it or you didn't, and I'd never yet met the woman who'd earned it.

"No, but when you talked about her—which was almost never—it sounded like you didn't even like her much." He shrugged. "Maybe one of these days you should try meeting someone who is actually nice."

I snorted. And now that word—*nice*—made me think about Evie Bates. Again. "The guy Gina screwed was cheating, too. I met his girlfriend. I felt bad for her, you know? I took her out for a sandwich."

Andrew licked a drop of coffee from his lip and raised one eyebrow—a talent he had that I didn't. "Uh huh," he said.

"What?" I was instantly on the defensive. "What does *uh huh* mean?"

"You took the guy's girlfriend out for a sandwich. Because that's what you do, take strange women out for sandwiches."

"I wanted to cheer her up."

"Uh huh," he said again. He was such an asshole. "You trying to sleep with her?"

"No."

"Not even a little?"

"I took a woman out for a sandwich without trying to fuck her, Andrew. Not even a little."

"So you're going to try to fuck her next time, then."

I shook my head. "Dude, she doesn't even like me. There isn't going to be a next time."

He looked skeptical. "What does this girlfriend look like?"

I shrugged. "She's a redhead. She looked like a redhead." My brother was steepling his fingers together like a comic book villain and peering at me like he could read my mind, so I said, "Forget it, dickbag. She works in a bank. She's too decent for me. I just felt bad because he fucked her over, that's all."

Andrew was obviously of my gene pool, because he said, "So go put dog shit on his porch or a laxative in his morning latte. Gina, too. They both deserve it. *Then* try to sleep with the redhead. That's what I would do."

"You're a real role model, you know that?"

Andrew nodded solemnly. "I've taught you everything I know, little brother."

"Mom and Dad would be so proud."

We both laughed, because the idea of our parents being proud of either of us was ridiculous. Our parents had checked out after Andrew's accident—it was, apparently, too much for them to handle. There were never two more useless people than John and Rita Mason. The only thing our parents were good for was money, and plenty of it. We'd come into our trust funds at twenty-one, and they'd thrown even more money at Andrew after his accident, because he made them uncomfortable. Me, they just hated.

So my brother had a scheduled caretaker, cleaners, groceries delivered, a home that was fitted for a wheelchair—everything except two parents who gave a shit.

"You need anything before I go?" I asked him.

He stopped laughing and scratched his nose. "The cleaning crew comes today, but the groceries don't come until tomorrow, and I'm low on a few things."

So I took care of it. This was what we did, Andrew and me. I helped him out with the stuff he couldn't do, or couldn't do easily. He hated it, and sometimes he argued with me, but in the end he always gave in, because he knew I'd do it anyway. He knew I wouldn't quit.

Aside from taking care of Andrew, I wasn't good for much. I'd dropped out of my first year of college after Andrew's accident. I didn't work, because I needed to help him, and who the hell wanted to work anyway? I sure as fuck hadn't settled down. The first years after the accident had been so hard, and such a blur, that I'd kind of lost track of things. Now I was twenty-six, and instead of looking around and wondering what the hell I was going to do, I avoided the topic by doing what I'd been doing pretty much nonstop for five years: partying.

It wasn't that I had a lot of friends. Friends are people who know you, who really give a shit about you. No, I didn't have friends—but I had acquaintances. I was rich, I was good-looking, and I was always looking for a good time, so the good times tended to find me. I'd started by blowing off steam a few times after the accident and the end of my college career, and somehow I'd never stopped. It was a rare night that I didn't get at least one invite. And I usually agreed.

It wasn't the alcohol that drew me—I could take it or leave it. It wasn't the women either, though I usually had one hanging around. No, it was the distraction that I was addicted to. Disappearing into a crowd, letting it take over, becoming someone else —or no one at all—for a few hours, until I fell into my bed with exhaustion—*that* was what I wanted.

By the time I finished getting Andrew's groceries, I had two different party invites in my texts. I accepted both of them.

I wasn't going to think about Gina, or redheads in overalls. At least for a little while.

I went home to grab some sleep before the long night began.

SIX

Evie

I waited two days before I showed up at the boxing gym.

I liked to think I was playing it cool, but I admit it—I had to work up my nerve. The place was in one of the crappier parts of town, tucked in the corner next to a strip mall, and I knew it would be full of sweaty, threatening men. I'd never boxed before; I'd never hit anything, ever. So not only would I look like fresh meat, I'd also look like the rank beginner I was.

But I went. I had to work all day at the bank with Josh, and the experience made me feel restless and mad. Nick was right; I wanted to hit something. It might be therapeutic. So I brought my gym clothes with me to the bank. Then, feeling weirdly like a criminal, I changed into workout clothes after work and snuck out to go to the boxing gym before anyone could see.

The place was as run-down as I imagined, bigger than it looked from outside, with a sparring ring in one corner, a few workout and weight areas, and some open, matted spaces with punching bags hanging from the ceiling. There were a dozen guys there, of all sizes and colors, working out their sweaty, bulging muscles. They barely glanced my way when I walked in the door, and no one bothered catcalling me in my yoga pants and sweatshirt. I was relieved and a little miffed at the same time.

I noticed Nick immediately. It was five o'clock, and he was here, just like he said he'd be. He was on the mats, punching one of the bags, wearing black gym shorts and a gray T-shirt that was soaked through in a V on his chest and back. The edge of a tattoo showed past the sleeve of his T-shirt, dark on his bicep. I hadn't noticed that when I'd first met him, the night he'd punched Josh with his jacket thrown to the floor.

As if he had a sixth sense, he stopped what he was doing and turned to me. A look of surprise crossed his expression, and he waved me over.

I walked to him, trying to look cool and nonchalant. Because, holy fuck. Nick wasn't bulging with muscles like some of the guys here, but his body was lean and mean, his chest and stomach taut with muscle that I could see through the clinging t-shirt. Even his legs were sexy, his calves roped with muscle and fine hair. There was a sheen of sweat where his neck disappeared into his shirt, his brown hair was damp, and he still had that shadow of stubble on his jaw. His gray eyes were focused on mine like lasers as I approached.

"So you decided to get mad, huh?" he said as he pulled off the gloves he'd been wearing.

I tried not to watch in fascination as the tendons and muscles moved in his arms. "Sure," I said. "Here I am."

"I knew you'd show."

"Because you're so irresistible?" I dropped my bag at the edge of the mat.

He was looking me over, the same look he'd given me in the diner that had stripped me naked, but there was a thoughtful edge to his expression. "No. I'm not. You know that, redhead. I knew you'd show because Bank Boy pissed you off, and you want to hit him."

"You keep calling him Bank Boy," I said. "I work at the bank, too."

He shook his head. "You won't last."

"Excuse me?" Jesus, did everyone think I was hopeless at having a career?

"You don't belong there," Nick said, his look going up and down me again. That look should make me mad, but instead it made me weirdly breathless. "That body, in a suit? You'll quit. I'm calling it."

What about my body? Was he saying something good or bad? I couldn't tell. "You don't know anything about me."

"We'll see who's right," he said. "In the meantime, you came here."

"You said I have an anger management problem."

"Yeah. I think you should hit something."

"You?" I asked.

He laughed low, probably at the hopeful tone in my voice. And now I was turned on again. It was so strange, what he did to me. "You're dressed good enough," he said. "Take your sweatshirt and shoes off and get on the mat."

I pulled off my sweatshirt, toed off my sneakers, and fished a hair elastic out of my bag, swiping my hair back into a ponytail. "I've never hit anything before," I told him as I got on the mat, my blood pumping.

Nick took a stance square across from me, just out of reach. "Okay, throw a punch," he said. "Let me see your form."

I made a fist and punched the air.

He watched me carefully, even though my punch was laughable and my arm looked like spaghetti next to his. "You're punching up," he said. "You hit on an angle, you lose power and you put stress on your shoulder. You want to punch at shoulder level, never above it. Not right or left, but straight to keep the power focused. Try it again."

I did. "Can I punch you now? Or at least the bag?"

"Not yet, because you'll crack something. Turn your fist, rotate it." He demonstrated in slow motion. "Use your wrist. See? And your stance is all wrong. Put your power leg back."

I moved my feet, but he shook his head. "Here." He stood next to me and slapped the front of my right thigh impersonally. "Leg back. Heel up. This is a power stance." He took my hips in his hands and turned them, his big, warm grip making me jump, though he didn't seem to notice. "Turn your torso." He used the same warm grip on my shoulders, moving them just so. "Right arm back. Now you twist and hit in one motion, and the power flows from your feet up through your body and your arm. You feel that?"

I did. I felt everything, the power of my legs, the turn of my body, the jab of my fist. I could also feel the heat of his hands on my hips, as if he was still touching me. He was close enough that I could smell the tang of his sweat and I could see the way his biceps moved when he extended his arm. Good God. I was starting to get pleasantly wet, something I wasn't about to admit to him. "Now can I try the bag?"

He moved me over, his touch giving me the shivers again. "Just hit lightly. You don't need force. Practice the hit. Straight from the middle knuckle, not the fourth finger or the pinky. Go."

I hit it a few times, hearing the satisfying *smack* when my knuckles hit the leather, feeling the surprising jolt in my arm. "I like this," I said. "Now I know why you hit Josh."

"You bet your sweet ass," Nick said. "Now the cross."

He showed me the moves—cross, jab, uppercut. He showed me the stances, the body work—I had no idea that punching started with the feet—and made me get the form right before hitting the bag. I was sweating in my t-shirt by the end, but my blood was singing and I was having more fun than I could remember. And Nick hadn't even insulted me once. Maybe he was in a good mood after doing the Victoria's Secret model he was banging in my imagination.

"Okay, now we try the real shit," Nick said, picking up two big white pads and holding them up. "You try and hit a moving target."

I obediently faced him, getting in a stance. "Shouldn't I learn how to dodge?" I asked him.

"No, because I'm not fighting you. This is only about you kicking ass. Now go."

I advanced on him, throwing punches at the white pads as he moved them. He moved back, to the side, then closer again, making me learn to get my footwork right while moving. Sometimes I missed, or things landed sideways, but I landed a few hits before he stopped me. "Fine," he said. "You've got the hand placement, the wrist placement. Now gloves."

He put gloves on me and we went again. "Oh my God, this is awesome," I said as I smacked the pads over and over. "I can hit hard without worrying about my hands."

"Hit as hard as you can," he coached me as we moved around the mat, probably because my hardest punch was something he could barely feel. He still never made fun, though—not once. It was weird. I had no idea whether any of the big meatheads here were watching, or smirking, and I didn't care; I just wanted to hit those pads as hard as I fucking could.

"Shout," Nick told me after a few minutes, "when you hit. It makes you hit harder and it forces you to expel your breath. You'll see."

So I shouted *"Josh, you suck!"* as I threw another punch, and I felt it land with a satisfying thud. Sweat was beading on my forehead and my temples now, making loose strands from my ponytail stick to my neck. I felt exhilarated, powerful, like I could conquer anything. It was better than sex, at least any sex I'd ever had. "You humiliated me!" I shouted, hitting Nick again and again as he moved. "I trusted you! She's a piece of trash!" *Smack, smack.*

"Jesus, redhead," Nick said, provoking me. "You hit like a girl."

"I *am* a girl!" I shouted back at him, hitting harder. I was getting the form right now, and I could feel the power in my punches. The words were coming out of me in a rush, not stopping until they were done. I actually started picturing Josh's face on the boxing pads I was hitting. "We were supposed to get married!" I shouted as I punched him. "We were supposed to follow the plan. Now the plan is shit and I'm going to die an old spinster unless I date Dave from Client Management! And he has a kid and a bunch of baggage!" I stopped, out of breath. My back and shoulders were on fire. I'd be paying for this for days.

It was worth it.

Nick dropped the pads. "Well, fuck," he commented.

I stared at him. I had a sudden fantasy of walking up to him and kissing him. Ripping his shirt off, pushing him down on the mat, pulling his shorts off, and jumping him. Right here in the middle of the gym. Blowing off steam, you might say, in one big orgasm.

Oblivious, he stepped forward and took one of my gloves in his hand, unfastening the velcro tapes at my wrist. I stared at a drop of sweat in his clavicle as if hypnotized. *Sex,* my brain said senselessly. *Sex, sex, sex.*

He took off my other glove, and I raised my eyes to see him looking at me. His expression was unreadable.

"That's good for today," he said. "Let's go get a milkshake."

SEVEN

Nick

I changed into another t-shirt and a pair of jeans and met her by the front door, my gym bag over my shoulder. She had put her shoes back on but her hair was still tied back, that brown-red color that looked different under different light. I'd be having boner dreams for weeks remembering what she'd looked like throwing punches, all those curves alive and moving.

"Sorry," I said. "There isn't a women's changing room here."

She shrugged. "I'll be sweaty, I guess."

"I didn't shower. So we're both dirty."

She paused at the word. Then she frowned. "I'm not sure that's a good thing."

"Too bad," I replied. "Where we're going, it doesn't matter."

She hefted her bag. "Where are we going?"

I pushed open the door and led her down the street. "Papaya Hut."

"What is a papaya hut?"

"It's a place that makes the best milkshakes you've ever

tasted. And if you're worrying about fat, don't. I have no clue what they put in those things, but it isn't cream."

"Please," she said, catching up and following at my shoulder. "Do I look like a woman who worries about fat?"

"It's legal to have an ass, Evie Bates," I said, pushing open the door to Papaya Hut. "Some of us even like it. If someone tells you you're fat, now you know how to punch their teeth in."

She was quiet after that.

The Hut was just a long, narrow space with a counter along one wall below a hand-lettered menu. I chose the blueberry-flavored shake, and she picked chocolate. She was still quiet as we got our shakes and took two high-top chairs at a narrow counter by the window, watching the street go by.

"This is ridiculously good," she said, her eyes going wide as she sipped her shake. "I was picturing Josh's face when I was punching back there. Is that normal?"

"Considering I punched his actual face, it's pretty tame."

"I'm not usually aggressive." She glanced at my chest, then my shoulder, then away again, as if she couldn't meet my eyes. "Can I ask you something?"

"Okay," I said, watching her mouth as she sipped from her straw again. Force of habit. For a nice girl, she had a sexy mouth.

"You don't seem very torn up about it. The whole cheating thing." She paused. "Gina."

"We weren't dating very long," I said. "Being torn up isn't my thing. And it's different for guys. It's all about pride."

"Pride?"

"Sure," I said. "You really want to know?"

"I think so. Yes."

"We like to know our cock is the only cock. You know, King Cock. No other cock in the universe can compare."

She stared at me open-mouthed, her cheeks going pink. "King Cock?" she said.

I narrowed my gaze at her as my temperature went up, starting in my balls. "Say that again."

Her eyes went wide. "Oh, I don't think so."

"Seriously, Evie. Say that again."

She swallowed. "Are you flirting with me?"

Now I was watching her throat. "I don't flirt. Ever. There's no point."

She put down her drink, flustered, and licked her lip. I couldn't stop staring. Finally she looked me in the eye. "You really are a bad boy, aren't you? Like, the real thing."

"I don't know what that means," I said, my voice thick. "Does it mean I get in your pants?"

Her pupils were dark as she looked at me. "I think you're actually coming on to me," she said. "Your version of it, anyway."

Was I? I didn't know. All I knew was that if we fucked, it would be hot and hard and we'd both get off in minutes. "You want me to?" I asked her.

"I thought you didn't want in my pants," she replied. She lifted her chin a little. "I'm not your kind of woman, remember?"

Right. She was a good girl. I needed to behave. "And I'm not your kind of guy."

"Not even remotely," she said.

I'd heard what she said back at the gym about wanting to get married, wanting a schedule. No, I was definitely not her kind of guy. "You take my advice yet?" I asked her.

"I thought I just did," she replied, confused. "Coming to the boxing gym for my anger management problem."

"No, the other advice. To find someone to fuck."

The first time I'd suggested it, she'd been outraged. Now she looked out the window pensively and bit her lip. And something inside me woke up and roared to life. *She can't possibly have done it already. It's only been a few days. No fucking way. She would have—*

"No," she said.

The beast calmed down.

Evie looked at me. "Have you?"

I shrugged, as if this whole conversation didn't affect me. Jesus, I was losing my mind. "No."

Her eyebrows went up. "Really? I mean—I'm surprised."

I'd said I was considering it in the diner, but the fact was it hadn't even crossed my mind. I'd just been trying to shock her. "Why are you surprised?"

Now, finally, she looked slightly embarrassed. "Because I heard rumors about you."

"Yeah? They're probably wrong."

She worried her lip again. She was polite, and she didn't like to gossip. "I heard you come from family money," she admitted finally.

"Okay," I said grudgingly. "True."

"And you don't have a job and you party all the time."

"Also true."

"And you get a lot of women."

"Define 'a lot.'"

She shook her head. "Okay, I admit I didn't actually hear that last one. It was an educated guess."

"Where are you hearing this shit?" I asked. There was no way she was talking to Gina. The two of them didn't inhabit the same planet. I didn't blame her because right now I didn't want to inhabit Gina's planet, either.

She took another sip of her milkshake. "I heard it from Josh," she said.

The beast woke up again and growled. Fucking Bank Boy. She was talking to him? She was mad at him, but she hadn't answered the question when I'd asked if she was in love with him. Maybe she wasn't over him. Maybe she was hoping she'd get him back.

Why the fuck did I care?

"He knows a hell of a lot about me," I said, "but he doesn't know a fucking thing."

I must have sounded dangerous, because she put down her drink and stared at me. "He hates you," she said.

That didn't surprise me. Most people hated me, including my own parents. "Yeah? Why?"

"Because you punched him. You embarrassed him. You made him feel this big." She held her thumb and forefinger an inch apart. "He called me up. He told me to stay away from you. He thinks you're going to take advantage of me. He said you'd come on to me and take advantage of my hurt feelings—like I can't control myself. It was idiotic. I've never seen him so mad."

"Yeah?" I said again. She'd lost that hollowed-out expression she'd had in the diner, when she'd said she wasn't skinny or good-looking enough to deserve him. When she talked about how mad Bank Boy was, her brown eyes were lit up with pleasure.

So there was one favor I could do for her. Everyone has a special talent. Mine was pissing people off.

"Let's make him mad, then," I said to her. "I mean, really mad."

"Nooo," she said, drawing the word out as she looked at me warily. "We already said we aren't doing that."

That made me smile. "Evie," I said, "you don't get it. We don't have to fuck. Bank Boy already thinks we're doing it, or almost. We just have to make it look like he's right."

"And how do we do that?" she asked, her voice a little strangled.

I thought it over. I already had a few invites on my phone. "What are you doing tonight?"

She shrugged, the motion tight. She seemed to be holding her breath.

"Gina and I have a lot of the same friends," I told her. "One of them is throwing a party tonight. We go, we act like we're fuck-ing, and the gossip mill will do the rest. Gina will hear about it in minutes. That means Bank Boy will hear about it. Our work is done."

She thought about it. She wanted to do it, but she was waver-ing. I could practically see the argument in her head. "I have to go to work tomorrow," she said. "I can't stay out late."

It was Thursday. I always forgot, because I didn't have a job. "No problem," I said. "We stay just long enough to be seen."

She was still wavering. "You can't kiss me or grab me or anything," she said. "You know, to make it look convincing." She cleared her throat. "No making out."

I put my hand to my heart. "No making out. I swear."

"Then how will it look like—"

"Trust me," I said. "We show up together, I tell them we're dating, and it's done." I couldn't resist. "Unless, you know, you *want* to make out."

"I do not," she snapped. Then she ran a hand through her ponytail. "I can't believe I'm considering this. A bunch of people will think we're dating. It's, like, a lie."

"So? I'll just wait a few days, then tell them you dumped me." I leaned toward her a little. "When was the last time you went to a party, anyway? I told you, you're missing out. You should try having some fun."

For a second, something flickered in her expression. Tempta-tion. And, I thought, familiarity. Good girl Evie had been to a party before. Maybe not recently, but she had. Maybe a lot of parties. And she'd liked it. Good girl Evie had maybe done a few bad things in her time.

Then she closed her expression off and put on her pinched, nice-girl scowl. "Fine, jerkoff," she said. "I'll do it. But just for revenge. And I'm bringing mace."

"You really know how to show a guy a good time," I said. "I'll

EIGHT

Evie

There was too much sunlight.

I rolled over in bed. I was warm and comfortable, but there was something... wrong about this bed. Something unfamiliar. I rubbed my aching head and stared up at the ceiling, which was also unfamiliar.

It was not my ceiling.

This was not my bed.

My breath stopped in my chest as everything came back to me.

Last night. The party. Oh, God.

It was in a big house, and there had been a lot of people there. Interesting people and great music. There had been fruity drinks, and then shots. New Evie never did shots, but Old Evie... Old Evie came out after the third fruity drink, and downed all of them.

The night had gone downhill from there.

Nick had looked hot as hell in jeans and a leather jacket.

We'd acted like a couple, like we'd agreed to, sticking close, but he'd followed the rules. We played it just right, him leaning in to me, saying things in my ear, almost touching me, never going far. He'd introduced me to his friends, who had looked at me with raised eyebrows, because every single one of them knew who I was. Knew who I'd been dating until a few days ago.

It was perfect. We'd caused a quiet little sensation among those people. After the wound-up stress I'd been feeling, it was freeing, and I'd been excited and—okay—really turned on. And his friends were fun. And I'd had a few more drinks, and those shots, then we'd—and then we'd—

I sat bolt upright, making my brains slosh in my head. I was drunk last night, but not so drunk that I didn't remember. I remembered everything. And Nick and I—

Oh, shit.

I looked around. I started with the window, which showed the sun just coming up. Then the floor, which was strewn with clothes—Nick's jeans, his jacket, his motorcycle boots thrown in the corner. I very purposefully didn't look at the body next to me on the bed. If I didn't look, it wasn't happening.

Quietly, I lifted the covers and peeked down at myself. I was wearing underwear and a T-shirt—Nick's T-shirt. It was dark gray with a faded Harley-Davidson logo on the front. I remembered that too—spilling one of the fruity drinks on my shirt, so Nick had given me his to wear instead while he grabbed a shirt from the guy hosting the party. The fruity drink had soaked through the shirt to my bra, so I'd taken that off, too.

Yes, I had done that. I had taken off my freaking bra. At a party with a bunch of strangers and a hot, strange man. I could practically hear my mother screaming in the back of my brain. *Not again, Evie!*

Don't panic. Right? Just keep cool. So I'd danced braless at the party to House of Pain's "Jump Around," and then we'd gone to Josh's place, and Nick and I had toilet papered Josh's nice townhouse condo in his nice neighborhood and let the air out of the tires of his precious Mustang, and then I'd prank called him. And then we'd come back here, and we'd stripped and passed out, and now I was in bed with Nick Mason.

This was not a problem. Everything was fine. It was all *fine.* This could be contained.

Something landed on the bed, and I jumped. A dog—a tiny dog—climbed onto my lap and started lapping my face with its small, warm tongue. I sputtered and tried to push it away, but it persisted.

The memory came back from last night. The dog greeting us, Nick saying something about having to take her out. He'd gone out briefly while I stripped and got in bed. He said the dog was a girl, and her name was—

"Scout."

The voice came from the other side of the bed. A low growl, muffled by pillows. My whole body tensed, my pulse going crazy. *Do not look. You are not in bed with Nick Mason right now if you do not look. Do not—*

"Scout," he growled again. "Fuck off."

Scout did a happy jig at the sound of his voice, her buggy little eyes wide with bliss, her tongue lolling out. Her whole body shook with joy. I had never seen a Chihuahua in real life before. It was completely absurd.

"I'll feed you in a second," Nick said. "Just chill."

Scout sat next to my knee, placing her tiny bottom on the comforter and waiting, her tongue still out. She tried to be still.

The room went quiet again. Nothing changed. Because this was happening—I was really here.

I took in the bedroom. It was big and spacious, with a high ceiling—Nick lived in one of those loft places. There was the huge bed, and a window, and a single dresser, with clothes piled everywhere on the floor. The source of Nick's many worn and mostly unwashed T-shirts, I figured. The entire place screamed *Guy living alone.*

And the guy who lived here, alone, was still in the bed next to me.

I turned my head and looked at him.

He wasn't looking at me, thank God. Nick was lying on his stomach, sprawled out, his face buried in the pillows. The blanket partly covered him, but I could see one smooth, gorgeous shoulder blade, one spectacular bicep—both covered in an intricate pattern of ink. A toned leg was hooked over the edge of the blanket, his tawny skin contrasting with the white comforter. I could see his dark tousled hair, the back of his neck. And I could see—he was wearing boxer briefs. Black ones. Visible against the white of the blanket was one perfect, unbelievable male ass.

I stared at it for a minute, helpless and ass-struck. It was impossible not to stare. It really was that kind of ass.

Had we—? No. We hadn't had sex. My memory was clear. We might be in bed together, in our underwear, but nothing had happened. No kissing, no touching, no making out. For a self-professed dirty guy, Nick had followed the rules. In his own crazy way, he'd actually been a gentleman. A hot, drunk, dangerous, gorgeous-assed gentleman.

Where the hell were my clothes?

And then it hit me. Work. It was Friday, and I had to go to work.

I must have made a sound, because from deep in his pillows, Nick said, "Evie. Are you panicking?"

Scout wiggled again at the sound of his voice and made a little whine.

"Um," I said, my voice hitching. "Possibly."

"Don't," he growled. "You remember what we did last night?"

"Yes," I said.

"You remember what we didn't do?"

I nodded, then remembered he wasn't looking at me. "Yes."

"You can get up," he said. "I won't look."

I slid my feet out over the edge of the bed and got up. Scout looked at me hopefully, but stayed next to Nick, since he was her food source. And, obviously, her religion. She looked at his unmoving form like the sun rose and set on it.

I walked around the bed, looking for my clothes. My stained shirt and bra were gone—I didn't think we even brought them home. I found my jeans, my socks, the ankle boots I'd worn. True to his word, Nick kept his face hidden in the pillows and didn't peek. I grabbed my clothes and ducked into the bathroom.

I steeled myself and looked in the mirror. I was a disaster: my hair on end, my makeup smeared, my eyes bleary. Worse, I was trapped in a man-bathroom with no supplies. I splashed water on my face, tried to finger-comb my hair. Now I just looked wet and awful. I looked around. The bathroom was spacious, with a big glassed-in shower and a large vanity counter. Nick had a very nice place, which meant he was probably rich, just like Josh had said. Normally I'd think it impolite to invade someone's privacy, but these were extreme circumstances. I pulled open one of the vanity drawers.

Condoms. It was full of condoms.

I slammed it shut, panicking. Jesus, how many condoms did one man need? I obviously wasn't the first woman to wake up in his bed, though by the looks of it I was the first one he hadn't had sex with.

That thought made me queasy for reasons I didn't want to explore, so I pulled open the next drawer. Hair gel—Nick didn't wear hair gel—and shaving cream. A stick of deodorant. A tiny black comb, which I scraped through my hair. I didn't see any evidence of Gina here—no leftover makeup, no Tampax. I wondered if she'd stayed over often.

The third drawer was the jackpot: a tube of toothpaste and an unopened spare toothbrush. I ignored the fact that the toothbrush was probably kept for his one-night stands and tore it open, quickly brushing my teeth.

I was just spitting and rinsing when I heard my cell phone ring in the bedroom. I must have left it on the floor. I had no idea who was calling me this early, and then I heard Nick's voice: "Evie's phone. Hello?"

Oh, no. He didn't.

"This is Nick," he said, obviously answering the other person's question. "Who's this? Oh, hey. She's in the bathroom. She just got up."

I had a terrible, terrible feeling of dread down my spine.

"No," Nick said. "I'm not the nice man from the bank."

Oh, shit.

Mom.

I dropped the toothbrush and ran out of the bathroom, leaving my clothes on the floor. Nick was lying in bed, on his back now, the covers pushed off him, propped up on the pillows, my phone to his ear. Scout had pressed herself into his armpit. I ignored the jaw-dropping sight of his boxer-brief-clad body and drew a line across my throat. The universal sign for *Cut it out.*

Nick saw me and frowned. "Sorry, but the nice man from the bank is an asshole," he said in his bar-band voice. "He cheated on her."

I launched myself onto the bed and grabbed for the phone.

I landed on his hard body, and he didn't even flinch. He just kept his grip on the phone as Scout jumped up and ran to safety. "Stop!" I hiss-whispered at him.

"Where are we?" he said, echoing my mother's question. "My place, I guess. In my bedroom. Who am I? I'm—"

I wrenched the phone away from him. "Mom!" I said into it,

"Who," my mother said, her voice breathless with shock. "Who... is *that man?*"

How to explain my mother? She was the nicest, kindest person I'd ever known. She was sweet and gentle and a great mother. She was also stuck in a time warp, where modern dating didn't happen. Nothing about my current situation—literally nothing—would make sense to her. "It's... it's no one, Mom. It's nothing."

Nick raised his eyebrows at that, and I realized I was lying on him. Directly on top, straddling his hips. He was freaking sculpted, hard as marble. And I was pressing against... I could feel... He gave me an amused smile, like he was watching me figure it out, and I pushed off him, using my free hand as leverage against his shoulder. The hot, gorgeous skin of his shoulder.

"That was not no one," my mother said in my ear. "Evie, it's seven thirty in the morning and you're with a man. A man who is not your boyfriend. I don't understand what's going on."

"Nothing's happening," I tried to explain, disentangling myself from the bedsheets and running for the bathroom again. I gave him a pretty good show of my backside as I went. I realized I was dressed a lot like Gina had been the other night, except the shirt was Nick's, I had panties on, and my ass was a lot bigger than hers. So maybe not quite as sexy. "I mean, nothing happened," I said, closing the bathroom door behind me. "He's just a guy I know. We were just sleeping."

God, that sounded like every lame excuse made to a mother since the beginning of time. Except it was true.

"Evie." My mother sounded confused and disappointed at once. She didn't mean to be judgmental, I knew—she just didn't get it, and the last thing I wanted to do was explain modern sex lives—*my* sex life—to my mother. "What was he saying about Josh? Are you not with him anymore?"

"No, I'm not," I said. Normally, I would have waited until at least Christmas to break this to her, then say it had happened months ago. Thanks a lot, Nick. "He, um, he found someone else. And he was dating her behind my back." I used the word *dating* instead of *fucking*, because I had never used the word *fucking* in front of my mother in my life. "So it's over."

"I can't believe that. Are you sure it's true? It's so strange. He seemed like such a nice man. I had high hopes for you two."

Marriage, babies—that was what relationships were for in my mother's world. Josh had seemed like a good prospect for both. "Yeah, well, I guess not," I said.

"You seem to have... found someone else, though. And I don't mean to pry, but... already?"

"No, Mom, I told you, he's just—"

"No one," Mom said. "That's what you said. But I know you, Evie. If you're in a man's... *bedroom*"—she had to force the word out, it was so shocking—"at seven thirty in the morning, it's because you're very serious about him. It's because you have feelings. That's the kind of girl you are. That's how I raised you."

I closed my eyes. "Oh, God, Mom."

"Bring him to dinner on Sunday," Mom said. "I want to meet him."

"No way," I said, my panic rising even higher. "Absolutely not."

"Well, I'm cooking for four," Mom said. "That's what I was calling you about. I was asking if you were going to bring Josh on Sunday. I was hoping to catch you before work. But now you're bringing—what did he say his name was?"

"Mom, please."

"Evie." My mother was never stern or angry, but for some reason when she said my name like that, I always caved. "This is surprising, I admit, but I wasn't born yesterday, you know. This young man is obviously very important to you. Tell me his name and bring him to dinner."

"His name is Nick," I said weakly.

"Five o'clock on Sunday," Mom said. "I hope he's hungry."

NINE

Nick

While Evie hid in the bathroom, trying to explain me to her mother, I got out of bed, pulled on some sweatpants, and fed Scout. She did another happy jig around her kibble bowl—happy jigs were Scout's specialty—and dug in, pulling each kibble out one by one and dropping it on the floor before eating it.

I put on some coffee, made toast, poured some juice. I wasn't too hung over, because I'd had less to drink than Evie did. Someone had to keep their head, and last night, it wasn't Evie.

My instinct had been right. Evie knew how to party, and she'd learned it somewhere. I wondered where.

Eventually she came out of the bathroom. She was dressed— no more sexy, curvy ass on display, though it was burned into my memory now—and she still had my shirt on. She had no bra on, I knew. I had spent a lot of time with braless Evie, considering I'd just met her. I approved. Her tits were smoking hot under there.

"You answered my phone!" she said, her cheeks flushed.

I had. Why had I done that? Curiosity, maybe. Also, I had

half hoped it was Bank Boy calling. "It was just your mom," I said. "No big deal."

"No big deal!" She closed her eyes and pinched the bridge of her nose, and I realized she had her uptight expression back on, her jaw tight, her brows furrowed. That expression had disappeared right before the shots last night, and I didn't like the fact that it was back. "My mother doesn't understand."

"Understand what?" I asked, pushing a piece of buttered toast across the counter at her. "That her grown up, single daughter might fuck a guy? It seems pretty understandable to me."

"I did *not* fuck you," she said.

"Believe me, I know."

"She thinks I'm bringing you to dinner on Sunday! I was supposed to bring Josh, and now somehow I'm bringing you!" She glanced away, panicked. "It's fine," she said. "I can control this. I'll just make up an excuse."

"Wait a minute." I leaned a hip against the counter. "Why am I coming to dinner? You actually said yes?"

"No. I didn't. I mean, I said—" She blew out a breath. "I didn't say anything, and she just assumed you're coming. That's what she does." Her gaze traveled down my bare chest, my stomach, and sort of froze there, distracted. Then she pulled herself together and dragged her gaze away. "It's a bad idea, right? Like, really bad."

"Yeah I'd fucking say so," I said.

She pulled her gaze back up to my face. The corner of her mouth twitched. "Never been to a girl's mom's for dinner before, huh Nick?"

That was putting it mildly. I'd rather go to Guantanamo Bay. "No," I said.

"Yeah. You're right. I'll just tell her you have leprosy. Or that you're an astronaut, and you took a five-year mission to Mars. Otherwise she'll bug me about you until Christmas."

"Or just say *Hey, Mom, I'm a grownup, none of your business,*" I said. "What does it matter what she thinks?"

That just made Evie look panicked again. "What my mother thinks is important," she said. "You don't understand."

She had sounded like a normal enough lady to me. But I knew nothing about having parents, since mine never talked to me if they could help it. "Never mind," I said. "I'm not the guy to ask for advice. Do you have anything on your phone from Bank Boy?"

"No," she said, taking a bite of toast. "Why?"

"That's what last night was about, right?" I said. "Making him jealous? I think we did a pretty good job, considering we didn't even make out."

Her cheekbones flushed red again, and I knew she was remembering last night, just like I was. We'd put on a hell of a good show. We'd been close, flirty, intimate. It had been very relationship-y. I hadn't thought it would be fun, but with Evie—especially drunk, relaxed Evie—it was easy. I knew that the Asshole News Network had been busily broadcasting everything to Gina. I already had six texts from her on my phone, but I didn't tell Evie that.

"It was pretty good, I guess," Evie allowed, swallowing her toast. "We really did toilet paper his place, didn't we?"

"Your idea," I pointed out.

She bit her lip. "And we let the air out of his tires, and I really did call him at three a.m. and make porn moans into his answering machine. Right?"

"Also your idea." A pretty funny one, in my opinion.

"And now I have to work with him."

"Not if you call in sick. Or quit."

"I can't do that. You don't understand anything, do you?" She was probably right about that. I'd understood the girl who did shots and made porn moans into the phone, but I wasn't sure I understood this version of Evie, wild-eyed and panicked like someone might brand an A on her forehead. "Right," she said to herself. "I've got this under control. I really do." She checked the clock on her phone. "Speaking of which, I'm almost late."

"You can't go to work yet," I said. "I can see your boobs."

"What?" She stared down at herself in alarm, as if she'd actually been topless this whole time and never noticed.

"I mean that you have no bra on," I said. I pointed. "They're, like, right there." And fuck, I wished I could look at them. But I kept that to myself. *This is Evie. She's nice. Be nice.*

"Shit," she said, crossing her arms over her chest, though it was a bit late for that. "I have to be at work in twenty minutes. What do I do?"

"Hold on." I went to my closet and, way in the back, found a jean jacket that used to be Andrew's. Andrew wasn't as small as Evie, but he was a little smaller than me. "Here," I said, bringing it out to her.

"Thank God for casual Friday," she said, putting it on. Now her boobs were covered, and she looked sexy and badass. Red hair, jeans, boots, Harley shirt, jean jacket. Jesus Christ. "Is it awful?" she asked me.

"No," I said, staring. I cleared my throat. "Not awful." *Pull yourself together, Mason.* "Do you need a ride?" She didn't have her car here, because we'd taken Uber everywhere last night.

"No, thanks," she said. "I gotta go."

"Make sure you tell Bank Boy how good I was," I said as she rushed to the door. She glared back at me, and I put my palms a foot apart, like a measurement. "This big, okay? I can send you a dirty text if you want."

"Are you always like this?" she asked.

"It's a condition," I said. "My big dick drains all the blood from my brain."

But she'd slammed the door behind her, and she was already gone.

TEN

Evie

Everyone stared when I walked in to work.

Everyone.

I felt my cheeks burning as I booted up my computer and logged in while someone unlocked the front doors. "What is it?" I murmured to Dar, who was sitting in the cubicle next to me. She had on a pressed button-down shirt and khaki pants. "Do I look that bad?"

"Bad?" she said, staring me up and down. "Evie, you look hot. I mean, *hot*."

"Stop it," I hissed. "I do not."

"You do," Dar said. "This is casual Friday at a whole new level. James in Customer Relations just about choked on his muffin when you walked by. And the guy fixing the photocopier has a hard-on."

I looked down at myself. "It's just a t-shirt and a jean jacket."

"Sweetie, this is a *bank*. I'm dressed daringly, and these are Dockers."

It didn't take me long to realize she was right. I could see it in people's faces. Male customers gave me a goggle-eyed glazed look; female customers just looked at me wide eyed, like *What the hell?* I had been afraid that everyone would know this was a walk of shame outfit: no makeup, no bra, man's t-shirt and jean jacket, last night's jeans and boots, hair fixed by some guy's comb. Instead, I seemed to give off a rock star I-don't-care attitude, like I was Pat Benatar in a 1980s video.

Or like I was Old Evie.

The Evie from high school, and that crazy first year of college, had worn a walk of shame outfit more than once. She'd slipped home at four a.m., her panties long gone from under her skirt. She'd lied about going to friends' houses and snuck off to parties instead. She'd come home with her hair smelling of hairspray and cigarette smoke, her breath smelling of vodka and bad decisions. She'd snuck a trip to the doctor's for birth control, and another trip to the drug store for condoms—which her mother had found, one disastrous morning, under the bed while she was cleaning.

Old Evie had been fun, but she'd gone too far, too. Done genuinely stupid things. One of the things that New Evie understood, now that those days were gone, was that trying some drug you didn't understand, or giving a guy a blow job in a closet on a dare, were not things you did when you had confidence and self-esteem. They weren't the way you gained, them, either. They were things you did when a tiny voice inside you, buried deep but never entirely silent, quietly told you to hate yourself. And when you banished that voice, you didn't do those things anymore.

Last night hadn't been like that. I hadn't heard that old voice, that I'd left behind for so long. I'd stayed in the realm of fun, without crossing the line into stupid. And Nick had something to do with that. Nick seemed to know instinctively where that line was.

But it was still far, far too close to Old Evie for comfort.

This is not me, I thought frantically as I served customers, trying to act casual and totally unsexy. *I am not this woman. I am not.* I sat unnaturally still, so my nipples would stop rubbing against Nick's t-shirt beneath the jean jacket. *I work at a bank. This is normal. Everything is under control.*

At eleven my phone vibrated in my purse, and between customers I surreptitiously checked it, keeping the phone under my desk so no one could see. It was a text from Nick. Without thinking, I tapped it.

Dear God.

Too late, I remembered his words: *I'll send you a dirty text if you want.* I didn't know he *meant* it.

He'd sent me a selfie. He was lying on his sofa, with Scout tucked under his arm. He was shirtless, holding the phone's camera above him, looking up into the lens. I'd seen that amazing chest and stomach a few hours ago, and I stared now, just as stupefied as I'd been then. The look in his eyes was mischievous and filthy. His free hand was hooked into the waistband of his sweatpants, tugging it down. Just a little. Just... a... little...

Last night was fucking awesome, he'd written. *Thinking of you, babe.*

I stared at that photo, my nipples hard under the jacket again. And there was a minute, a long aching minute, when I wished all of it was real.

That I'd gone out with Nick last night and we'd had fun, and then wild, dirty sex.

That I was wearing this walk of shame outfit because I'd spent the night having orgasm after filthy orgasm.

That he was texting me now because he was thinking of me, and not because he was faking. And when I finished work, I'd go back to his place yet again, and pull off my shirt, and pull down his sweatpants like he was doing now, and then we'd—

"Jesus, Evie, for fuck's sake."

I jumped and slammed the phone down onto my thigh. "What?"

Josh was standing next to my cubicle, looking over my shoulder. He was wearing Dockers and a navy blue flannel shirt for Casual Friday. He had bruises under his eyes, like a raccoon, from where Nick had punched him. His eyebrows were lowered, his arms crossed over his chest as he stared at me, livid. "Dirty texts at work?" he said. "From *him*?"

That made me scowl, even though the dirty text was supposed to be for his benefit. "You didn't have to look over my shoulder, you know. Which makes it none of your business."

He didn't budge. "We need to talk. In private."

RELUCTANTLY, I stood and walked with my cheating ex-boyfriend down the hallway to the lunch room. I'd always thought Josh was good-looking, and except for the bruises, he was as good-looking as ever. But now I could barely look at him. I kept a good eight inches away from him, out of the zone of any possible touching, as if we were two magnets pointed the wrong way. People stared at us as we walked down the hall, and I felt my stomach churn.

There was no one in the lunch room, thank God. Once we were through the door, I broke away from him, putting space between us as I opened one of the cupboards and took out a tea bag from my work stash. "So?" I said, trying not to let my voice shake. "What do you want?"

"Last night," Josh said, his voice accusing. "What the hell were you doing?"

"I don't know what you're talking about," I said, putting water in my mug.

"Toilet papering my place? Calling me to make disgusting noises?" He sounded angry, but I kept my back turned so I wouldn't have to look at him. Still, he railed on. "I was late for work because of those stupid tires. You went to some party with Nick Mason, and now he's naked on your phone. Evie, I warned you about him."

It had worked then, our little jealousy scheme. "Yeah, you did warn me," I said to Josh, shoving my mug in the microwave so hard the water sloshed. "I heard you."

"I mean, what is going on?" he said, still behind me because I wouldn't look at him. This lovely, uptight rant was making my hangover headache pound in my temples. "This isn't you. Gina thinks you're doing this just to get back at me, and I think she's right."

That made me turn around. "I do not," I said, my voice low and more dangerous than I'd ever heard it, "give a shit what Gina thinks. Is that clear?"

Josh looked startled, but he shook his head. "I'm sorry about what happened," he said. "I already said that. But Evie, there's no reason to go around putting on an act—"

"Maybe it isn't an act." The microwave beeped, and I turned around and yanked my mug from it, throwing my tea bag into the hot water. I had no lunch with me, so this would basically be my sustenance for the day, as gross as it was. "Maybe this is the way I am. You just never saw it."

"Evie, come on. We dated for four months. I know you pretty well."

I thought about the girl who'd been so eager to go out with him, so happy she'd been picked. It had been a sign, I was sure, that I was putting my past behind me. That I was finally worth something. I thought about that now—only four months ago—and it made me feel faintly sick. Why had I thought that? That a clean-cut guy, a nice boyfriend, would change who I was for the better? How completely deluded had I been?

"No," I said to Josh. "I don't think you know me at all."

He was watching me, his expression hard to read past the bruises on his face. But it looked a little like disdain. And I wanted to use my newfound fighting skills and punch that expression right off him.

"Evie, come on," he said. "Get real." Like he knew everything. Every fucking thing.

"This is real," I said. "You saw that text. I am..." I forced the words out. "I am *sleeping with* Nick Mason. What do you think of that?"

Technically, it was true. We'd slept. Quite comfortably. Me, and Nick, and Nick's gorgeous butt in his boxer briefs. And the other parts I'd felt when I'd jumped on him this morning. Because when I was in bed with a hot bad boy, that's what I did. I slept, because I was too chicken to do what I wanted.

"Since when?" Josh snapped, his cheekbones going red with anger.

Oh, now I had him. "Since that first night," I lied, inspired. "When I left with him. And every night since. We can't keep our hands off each other. We're in bed all the time. I have so many orgasms I can barely stand it."

"So that's it?" Josh said. "You just jumped into bed with some dirtbag? You think you're that kind of girl?"

The hypocrisy of it—the absolute, utter hypocrisy of Josh disapproving of my fictional sex life after cheating on me—made me gape at him for a second. I always knew there was a double standard, but I'd never seen it this close. "What kind of girl do you mean?" I said. "Sexy? A girl who likes hot guys? A girl who picks her own sex partners? A girl with *spark*?"

"I hope you don't think he's marriage material," Josh said

"Ask any of the girls he's dumped. He's the farthest thing from it. You're fooling yourself, Evie."

"I am not looking for marriage material!" I shouted. Dimly, I thought that everyone in the office could probably hear us. But I couldn't bring myself to care.

"Are you kidding?" Josh shot back. "It's written all over you. I had to meet your mother the first week. We were practically picking out venues and rings. I had to go looking just so I could feel alive again. And the next day you meet Mason, and now you come to work dressed like a slut."

That was when I threw the tea cup at him, and watched the hot water splash all over the wall.

ELEVEN

Evie

They sent me home. *Take some personal time,* my manager said. *Take next week off. Rethink things, Evie, before you come back.*

It was said like they cared, but I knew what it was—a warning. I was almost-fired. *Get your shit together, or don't come back.* That was the message.

They didn't send Josh home.

Tears burned behind my eyes. I swallowed them. I went home to my apartment, stripped my clothes off, and took a long, hot shower. Then I put on a cami and a pair of boxer shorts and crawled into bed. I lay on my back, staring at the ceiling and thinking.

You fucked it up, Evie. Again.

This was exactly like the first time I'd screwed up my life. The first two times, actually. The first was when I'd crashed and burned in high school, failing so many classes that I had to go to summer school my final two years to barely scrape by. The second time was when my mother had scrimped and saved to send me to college, and I'd promptly flunked out after two semesters. Yeah, that was my stellar past.

I had no college degree, no nothing. After the second flame-out, I'd worked a menial job in a bakery for three years, getting up at four a.m. to bake before the place opened at six. It didn't matter that I actually liked baking—it wasn't a career job. It was minimum wage and demeaning. Other people my age were doing things, traveling, getting degrees, finding partners, putting their lives together, and I'd just baked while striking out with boyfriend after boyfriend. Worse, I'd thrown my mother's hard-earned money down the drain, and I'd probably disappointed my dad from the grave, too. If there was a poster girl for going nowhere fast, I was her.

The bank job had changed that. It had been my big break, when they took a chance on me. Nice people, regular hours, high heels, more money. Possible promotion, even. And then, once I started working there, I'd met Josh, and he'd changed it, too. A good job and a good boyfriend—the new, improved me thought I'd finally been on track.

Now I'd lost both. The boyfriend, for sure, and I wasn't an idiot. I knew that if I still had my job, it wouldn't be for long.

My expenses weren't high, but my savings were meager, and if I was unemployed, they wouldn't last long. I wouldn't even be able to afford my shared apartment after a few months. Maybe I could clean up my act, go back to the bank, beg them for forgiveness. But then I'd be back to working with Josh every day.

Maybe I could swallow my pride, my self-worth, and do it. Maybe I should, even though I'd have to see Josh all the time. Maybe even with Gina. Would I see him with Gina?

They weren't very discreet, Dar had said.

I frowned at the ceiling. That still didn't sit quite right. I'd worked at the bank for months, and I'd never seen Gina there. How were Josh and Gina not very discreet?

Then, Josh. *Don't say anything at work.* And his little freak out. *Who told? What did they say?*

I'd thought it strange that he was worried about our coworkers knowing about Gina, especially if he wasn't discreet in the first place.

Unless... it wasn't Gina he was worried about.

A dark, creeping suspicion made its way up my spine.

Still lying on my back, I picked up my phone and called Dar's cell phone.

"Hey," she said, her voice hushed. "Hold on." I heard shuffling, then the familiar squeak of the women's room door at the bank. Every woman who needed a private conversation, away from management, used that women's room. "Okay," Dar said, her tone more normal now. "Jeez, Evie, I heard what happened. I'm so sorry. Are you okay?"

"I'm all right," I said, though I didn't really think I was. "I just lost my temper, you know? It's for the best that they sent me home for a few days. I don't think I can work with Josh right now."

"I totally don't blame you," Dar said. "This fucking sucks. If it's any consolation, I think he's an idiot to lose you over her."

"Thanks," I said. It wasn't much of a compliment, considering Dar had known Josh was cheating on me for God knew how long, but hadn't seen fit to tell me. Still, I'd called her for a reason. "Can you just tell me one thing? Then I won't suck you into my drama anymore."

"Sure," she said, though she didn't sound sure at all.

"Just tell me how they met."

She sighed. "I think it was around Valentine's Day. You remember when we had those paper hearts up everywhere, and a cake for all the customers?"

"Yeah," I said as the air slowly closed off in my throat. "I remember."

"Well, all I know is that Gail sent Alison to pick up the cake, and Josh went with her. And they were gone for *two hours*. It was so strange, everyone had started talking about it, but when they came back they acted all casual, even though everyone knew. And after that, it got out through the grapevine that they were seeing each other, so I knew I guessed right."

Alison. She was talking about Alison Shepard, another teller. She thought Josh was cheating with Alison, not Gina.

Or he was cheating with Alison *and* Gina.

There were two of them.

Where the hell had I been on Valentine's Day? I remembered. Sitting in my cubicle, doing my job as always. Oblivious to what was going on around me because I thought it completely innocent that my boyfriend had gone to pick up the cake.

"Okay," I said. I had that crazy, curiously numb feeling I'd had when I'd walked into Josh's apartment and seen him with Gina. Like this was happening to someone else. "I guess I just wanted to know how it happened. Thanks for letting me know."

"If there's anything I can do—"

I hung up. I wasn't crying. I wasn't even hyperventilating. I felt like someone had shot me in the arm with Novocaine. Through the blankness, a thought bubbled up. Something I realized I wanted.

I called Nick Mason.

"Yeah?" he said. He sounded like maybe he'd been sleeping. It was two o'clock in the afternoon. Then again, he usually sounded like that. And I was in bed in my underwear, so I couldn't throw stones.

"It's me," I said.

"I know, redhead. You at work?"

Why did I like it when he called me that? When he didn't use my name? He knew my name—he'd said it plenty of times.

But when he called me *redhead*, I got chills up my spine. "I'm not at work," I told him. "They sent me home."

There was a pause, because even Nick knew that was bad. "What happened?"

"Josh saw your text. He started an argument. I threw a mug of tea at him. So here I am."

"Fuck," he said softly. "It wasn't supposed to happen that way. Jesus, Evie, I'm sorry."

He was. That was the thing about Nick—deep down, buried below the asshole surface, was an almost-nice guy who took the time to teach me to box and who didn't want me to get fired.

But I didn't want that nice guy right now.

"It's okay," I said to him. "They gave me a few days off. I'm sort of maybe fired, but now I don't have to work with Josh every day."

"What the hell did he say to you?" Now the growly voice was back, and I got another shiver.

"He called me a slut," I said.

"He fucking called you what?"

More shivers. "Yeah. I got slut-shamed, and I didn't even get to have sex. Oh, and he's cheating with a woman at work as well as Gina, so he completely fucked me over. I'm not having a really good day."

He took a second to acknowledge this. "You want to hit something?" he asked.

"No," I said. "Not this time. I want something else."

"Yeah? And what is that?"

I took a breath. "You said something about dirty sex when we first met."

There was a pause. Barely a heartbeat long, but it was there. "Did I?"

"You did," I said. I was picturing him in my mind right now. Lying in bed, mostly naked, like the photo. Oh hell, that photo.

"You said that I'm nice, and that you're too dirty for me, and that's why we can't fuck."

Another heartbeat of surprise at my foul language. But Nick, of all people, knew exactly where I was going. "Yeah," he said. "I said that."

"I've decided I hate being nice," I told him. "I want to do things your way. I've had the world's shittiest day, and I think some dirty, dirty sex would make it better. And I think you're the guy to provide it."

This was it. The moment when he could laugh at me. Make me feel stupid or ugly. Tell me I wasn't sexy or attractive. Tell me to leave him alone.

Instead, he said, "Right now?"

My heart leapt in my chest. It freaking *leapt*. "Yes. Right now."

He made a rumbling, thinking sound, a little like *hmmm* but mixed with an exhale. "That might be a shitty idea, Evie."

"It isn't a shitty idea," I said, because it wasn't. It really wasn't. "It's a good idea."

"You're kind of vulnerable, or something. Emotional or some shit."

"I am not emotional!" The panic in my voice made that a lie, but I didn't care. "I'm perfectly sane, and I need some dirty sex!"

"See, that right there," he said. "That's emotional. We fuck right now, and we do it dirty, you'll probably change your mind and regret it."

"You have got to be kidding me!" I slapped a frustrated hand down on the mattress beside me. "This is a booty call, Nick! A serious one! No strings attached!"

"And I very much fucking appreciate it," he said. "But you're all twisted up and turned around. And dirty sex with me is very fucking filthy. That's a bad combination. It isn't going to work."

Why? Why was he being nice now, of all times? I was so

done with nice. "You're serious, aren't you?" I said. "You're turning me down."

He made a pained noise in his throat. "Yeah," he said. "I have to."

"Well, thanks for nothing!" I shouted at him, hurt now as well as angry. Had he ever turned Gina down? Who was I kidding? Of course he hadn't. "Take your chivalry and shove it!" I hung up the phone and threw it on the floor.

I pressed the heels of my hands to my eyes. This was my life right now. I couldn't even get the world's dirtiest guy to fuck me, and I'd been in bed with him just this morning. What was wrong with me?

If what you're doing isn't working, change it.

The words floated into my mind. Clear and simple. Had I heard them somewhere? Some self-help article? I had no idea, but there they were.

If what you're doing isn't working, change it.

Powerful and scary at the same time. Words that took courage.

My life wasn't working. My career, my love life, my sex life. None of it was working right now. What did I have to lose?

If what you're doing isn't working, change it.

It was time to admit that being nice wasn't working for me. At all.

Maybe it was time to change it.

TWELVE

Nick

"It's official," Andrew said. "He can't get out of this one. I think Lightning Man is fucked."

"He's not fucked," I said, taking another swig of beer. "He'll get out of this, just like he gets out of everything else."

"No way." He leaned forward, his computer stylus pen in hand, and fixed something tiny on the screen that I couldn't see. "Temptus has made the entire planet of Pluto into a nuke and is hurling it at Earth. How the hell is Lightning Man supposed to get out of that?"

I didn't know, actually. It was Saturday night, and we were sitting in Andrew's living room, each of us with a beer in hand. I was on a chair with my feet up, a notebook on my lap as I jotted down sketches and ideas. Andrew was at the computer, his Illustrator program open, actually creating Lightning Man onscreen.

I may have been a party animal, I was a homebody one night a week: Saturday. My friends—acquaintances—didn't understand it, but I didn't give a shit. This was our ritual, Andrew and me.

Saturday nights, we'd hang out in his living room, drink beer, and make comics.

I didn't even remember how it had started. Sometime after his accident, I'd taken to coming up with outrageous comic stories by his bedside, and sometime after that Andrew had started drawing the stories I invented. During the long, thick fog of his recovery, after our parents had bailed on both of us, the comics were a way for us to keep each other company without actually having to talk. Because when we talked, we always danced around the real issues—or talked about them, which was way fucking worse. We were talked out. Making up the exploits of Lightning Man was better.

Now we'd graduated to making Lightning Man on a computer instead of a pad and paper. That was Andrew's talent, not mine. He could take up a stylus pen and do a computer drawing that knocked your socks off, while I could barely draw a stick figure. So I stuck to the storytelling part.

We didn't publish Lightning Man, not online or anywhere else. No one had ever seen Lightning Man except for Andrew and me. That was what kept him interesting—the fact that he was ours, and ours alone.

"Okay, genius," Andrew said now, quickly setting up the next panel. "Pluto, which is now a nuke, is hurtling toward Earth. What's next?"

I was already doodling a solution. This was how I plotted Lightning Man—I came up with an unsolvable problem, then pulled a solution out of thin air. Since no one was reading it, it didn't matter whether the plot was believable. "Well, here is Temptus's problem," I said, referring to our supervillain, who had horns and was always trailed by wisps of smoke in Andrew's drawings. "The distance from Pluto to Earth is so big, his nuke is going to take"—I looked it up on my phone—"twenty-three years to get here. So he has to send the nuke through a hole in the space-time continuum to get it here faster."

"Uh huh," Andrew said, already sketching Temptus in his sketchbook, his way of trying out ideas. Temptus was scribbling equations on a white board.

"When Temptus opens the space-time continuum," I said, "Lightning Man will jump into the rift, reversing the effects with his presence."

"That puts Lightning Man adrift in space and time," Andrew pointed out.

"Not if Thunder Boy is back at headquarters with a program that will pull Lightning Man out of the continuum, as long as he is pulled out before the rift closes. Which is ten seconds."

Andrew nodded as if this was an actual possibility. "Tricky," he said. "But Thunder Boy is a genius. What's going on with the redhead?"

For a second, I thought he was still talking about the comic. "What redhead?" I asked.

My brother turned from the screen and rolled his eyes at me. "The hot girl you took out for a sandwich, dumbass. That redhead."

Fuck. Evie. "Nothing is happening," I said, and I felt the pain of those words, right in my balls. *Nothing is happening*.

"Nothing?"

"It's possible I fucked it up."

Andrew looked surprised, though he shouldn't have. "It's *possible*? Fucked it up how?"

Just talking about this brought a tension headache to my temples. I had never done anything more difficult in my life than turn Evie down yesterday. But I couldn't think of what else I could have done.

No, that was a lie. I *could* think of it. And I did. A lot. But I still didn't think I was wrong.

Andrew was waiting for an answer, and I told Andrew everything, so I said, "I fucked it up by not having sex with her."

"What?" Andrew said. "I thought you weren't sleeping with her."

"I'm not. Thanks for the reminder of my blue balls, though. She asked, and I said no."

"Uh huh," Andrew said, disbelieving. "So the redhead asked you for sex."

"Yes." *I think some dirty, dirty sex would make it better. And I think you're the guy to provide it.* Damn, I would be hearing those words on my deathbed. When I would still be regretting saying no.

"And you turned her down," he continued.

"I had to," I explained. "She was only asking because she was emotional. She'd just been almost fired from her job, and she'd had a big fight with her douchebag ex. He wasn't only cheating with Gina, but someone else, too. She was in a crazy mood. She was up and down and sideways all at once."

Andrew scratched an eyebrow thoughtfully. "What did she do when you said no?"

"She got mad, and hurt," I said. Fuck, I hadn't meant to hurt her. That part stung. "She told me to take my chivalry and shove it."

"She told you that, and you still said no?" my brother said.

"It was bad," I admitted. "It was very fucking bad. Maybe I didn't handle it right. I have no idea. But having sex right then would have been worse." I didn't say the worst part: Sex, right then, would have ended us. That was the part I didn't say. Because it sounded ridiculous, not wanting to end something that didn't exist in the first place.

Andrew shook his head. "How you have so many women, and know so little about them, amazes me."

"Because I never *talk* to them, buttwipe," I said.

"So, talk to this one," he said. "Call her."

"And say what?"

He counted on his fingers. "I'm sorry, I hope you're okay, I think you're hot even though I totally fucking hurt your feelings. There's a starter script. Go from there."

"She'll get the wrong idea," I said.

"Like what? That you actually like her?"

I glared at him. Because yeah, that was what I meant. I didn't want her to know I liked her.

I didn't like her. It was just a revenge thing.

Except I sort of did. This was Evie. What was not to fucking like?

Jesus, I was a fucking mess.

"Fine," I said, like I was doing Andrew a favor. "I don't know why I take your advice about women, when you know even less about them than I do." I pulled out my phone and stood up. "I'll be back in a minute."

"Sure," Andrew said. "Take your time."

The fact that he was so agreeable probably meant that he had some secret way of listening in, but I couldn't be bothered with that right now. I stepped out onto his front porch and dialed Evie's number.

She answered, and there was a blare of sound, as if she was somewhere loud. "Nick!" she shouted over the noise. "Hi!"

She sounded panicked and relieved at the same time, which I didn't expect. "Evie?" I said. "Where are you?"

"I can't hear you," she said. "Hold on." I waited a second, but the noise didn't go down. It sounded like the pulse of loud dance music. "Shit, I still can't hear you," she said. "Let me—" The line went dead.

So much for playing it casual.

I couldn't let it go. So I texted her instead. *Where are you?*

Cintano's, she replied, naming a trendy downtown bar.

Known mostly for hookups, if you were a trendy kind of person. Which Evie wasn't. She was a lot of things, but trendy wasn't one of them.

Still, I had to ask the question. *What are you doing there?*

Her answer took a second. *You told me to find someone to fuck me,* she wrote. *And you won't do it. So here I am.*

I stared at the words with disbelieving eyes. Then I closed my eyes and tilted my head back.

Fuck. *Fuck.*

Why was I so stupid sometimes?

It was none of my goddamn business. She was right, I'd said no. Evie was free and single, and could go to Cintano's on Saturday night if she wanted. Pick up who she wanted. Fuck who she wanted.

Not my business at all.

Except Cintano's was a meat market. She didn't belong in a meat market, meeting those kinds of guys. Letting them buy her drinks and come on to her. Letting them touch her and take her home.

I didn't care. Nope. We'd been of some use to each other, gotten drunk for one fun night, and that was all. We weren't dating or fucking. We weren't anything, even though she'd tried.

She was at Cintano's on Saturday night.

The beast inside me roared to life again. Evie with her pretty red hair, her soft skin, her nice round ass, at Cintano's. Right now.

I should not fucking care about this.

The phone buzzed in my hand again. It was Evie.

Confession, she wrote. *It isn't going very well.*

Oh, fucking hell. That sealed it. *I'll be right there,* I texted back. *Don't move.*

"Hey!" Andrew said as I came back inside and put on my

leather jacket. He held up his hands. "What about bros before redheads?"

"Next time," I told him.

"Fine. But while you're gone, I'm going to draw Lightning Boy and Judy Gravity getting it on. And it's going to be *filthy*."

"Do not draw that," I shouted over my shoulder, and I banged the door shut behind me.

THIRTEEN

Evie

Confession. It isn't going very well.

I had never been to Cintano's before. But if a girl is going to try and get herself laid, she may as well go to the top place in town for it. On Saturday night.

This was the new me—or, should I say, newer than the last new me. I was going to be bold and sexy. Adventurous. But I was also going to be confident and in control. I wasn't going to be the sad-sack cheating victim Josh had made me out to be, or the pathetic hard-up girl who begged Nick Mason to have sex with her. I also wasn't going to be the boring bank teller with "marriage material" on an invisible sign over her head. None of the guys at this bar knew me, so I was going to be someone new, and sexy, and fun, just for one night.

Fuck Nick Mason and his stupid scruples. Just fuck them.

There were plenty of men in Millwood. Nick Mason wasn't the only one. I would go pick another one. Easy.

While my roommate Heather blared Howard Jones in her

room, I picked out a wrap dress from my closet: basic black, knee length to cover my ass, with a deep V neck. I added a silver necklace and a pair of heels. On a wave of inspiration, I picked up the jean jacket Nick had lent me and tried it on. The look was dressy and classy, overlaid with the sharp denim, and I liked it.

I was adjusting the jacket when I noticed something in the breast pocket. I pulled it out and found a business card. *Andrew Mason, programmer. Specializing in PHP.* There was a phone number and an email. Huh. Who was Andrew Mason? A brother or a cousin? The jacket was a too small to fit Nick, but it was definitely a guy's jacket, big enough to give cover to my ample boobs, though I had to roll the cuffs.

Whatever. Nick was a mystery in a lot of ways, but he wasn't one I was going to ponder tonight. I put the card back in the jacket pocket, blow-dried my hair, put on some makeup, and headed out.

I only had a mild panic attack when I got out of the Uber in front of the bar. And a second one—again, mild—as the bouncer waved me through. Oh, God, I was in Cintano's. To pick up. Right. Let's do this.

There was a dance floor, already full, ringed with tables, chairs, and booths in lots of dark nooks and crannies. A huge bar lined the back wall, lit with cunning little lights inside the bar and above it, so you could see what you were ordering and paying, but not a whole lot else. The whole place smelled like perfume, cologne, dank dance floor sweat, and sweet mixed drinks.

I walked to the bar and ordered a white wine. I was dressed to kill and obviously on my own—should I find a guy and talk to him? Or would he talk to me? Even in the bad old days I'd met guys through work, school, or friends, so I'd never done this before. But I got my glass of wine and nothing happened, so I sipped it like a loser, wondering what was next.

There was lots of traffic at the bar. The guys were dressed up—nice dress shirts, styled hair, some of them with necklaces or rings. There was a lot of cologne. They weren't the kind of guys I'd dated before, but they weren't hideous either, and that was what this night was about. Someone new. Someone different.

Too late, I realized why women tended to come to these places in groups. Right now even Dar, or Heather, my roommate, would be better than standing here like a stick.

"Hi," a guy next to me said. He nodded to me as the bartender slid his drinks to him.

"Hi," I said back.

"Nice night, huh?" he said.

"Yeah," I said.

He nodded again, picked up his drinks, and walked off.

That was when I started to panic. I wasn't feeling confident anymore. I looked down and realized I'd drunk my wine too fast, but I needed another glass, or I'd be standing here with nothing in my hand. So I ordered another.

I was about to pull out my phone and pretend to be talking to someone when another male voice said, "Hi."

I turned. This guy was all right: short dark hair brushed forward, a blazer and a shirt unbuttoned at the throat. I could work with this. "Hi," I said.

"You here alone?" he asked. I mostly got the words by lip-reading, the music was so loud.

I nodded in answer.

"Come sit with me and my friends," the guy said. "Let's hang out."

He pointed, and I looked past him. In a booth, watching us and nodding, were five other guys. Five. Two of them had back-ward baseball caps on. While the others weren't looking, one of them waggled his tongue at me.

Um, that was a lot of men. There was no woman in sight. "You have a lot of guy friends," I said.

"Come on," the man said, ignoring me. "You like to party? We like to party."

The guys in the booth waved. The tongue guy waggled his tongue again.

Great. I'd apparently replaced my Marriage Material sign with one that said *Please date rape me.* "I'm okay," I said, the all-time lame version of *No, fuck off* that every woman seems to use in a situation like this. "I'll just stand here."

"It's a good time!" the guy said, standing closer.

So I used the second weapon that women use in bars. "I have to go to the bathroom," I said, and walked away.

Should I actually go to the bathroom? Was he watching? Why did I care? I ditched my drink—that creep had probably roofied it—and kept walking toward the back of the bar. Operation Get Laid hadn't lasted fifteen minutes before a retreat to the ladies' room. I needed a break before round two.

Forty-five minutes later, I was sweaty, tired, and depressed. I was going to die without ever having sex again, and I had the creeping feeling that my hair smelled like cologne. I might have to burn this dress, which sucked, because I liked it. If this was the selection to choose from of the male of the species, I was totally doomed.

The crowd was a thick, solid wall of bodies now, and I was making my way slowly through it on sore feet to make an escape when my phone buzzed. I looked at the display. It was Nick.

I tried not to feel excited. I really did. But when I couldn't hear him over the pounding music, I had a moment of panic until my phone buzzed again with a text. *Where are you?*

I didn't know why he was asking. Did he care? He was probably at a party himself somewhere, like he was every night.

Maybe even with some girl he wasn't saying no to. *Cintano's,* I wrote.

What are you doing there?

That made me mad. He didn't have to know I was teetering on the brink of existential despair, so I wrote *You told me to find someone to fuck me. And you won't do it. So here I am.*

He didn't answer that. Maybe he didn't care. Maybe he was too busy with what's-her-name (I already pictured someone better-looking than me in my head) to use his thumb anymore. Too bad.

People bumped in to me, and someone stepped on my foot. I wasn't cut out for this; I had to face it. The fight went out of me as I looked at the long distance from me to the faraway exit. *Confession,* I typed to Nick almost without thinking. *It isn't going very well.*

I'll be right there, he wrote back. *Don't move.*

My stomach flipped. In that split second, I forgot about my shitty situation and our fake relationship and our almost-fight, because *Nick was coming to get me.*

It wasn't that I couldn't get out of here on my own; I could. But right now, in the middle of this crowd, I was so lonely I wanted nothing more than to see a familiar face. *His* face.

I didn't know exactly where he'd find me, so I spent twenty more minutes making my way through the crowd toward the door. My hair was sticking to my neck and my bra was digging into my ribs under the wrap dress. I had just made it to the thinning crowd near the door—and had gulped down a precious breath of fresh air—when I did, indeed, see a familiar face. Just not the one I wanted.

Gina was wearing a red dress that hung off her perfect frame like a tunic, barely covering her ass. Her hair was long and glorious down her back, and her legs went for miles before ending in three-inch heels. She was with two other women, and she was rifling through her tiny clutch for something. Then she looked up and saw me.

I didn't know what to do. I was sort of frozen. What I really wanted was to turn and run away, but that would look bad. I could put my chin up and look snobby, maybe, but even I knew my face wasn't very convincing that way. So I just settled for standing there, once again like a loser, while she came toward me.

"Where is he?" she said. Her perfectly made-up eyes were staring at me like lasers, her nicely glossed lips terrifying in their pouty beauty.

Nick? Did she mean Nick? Why was she asking about him? "He's coming," I said.

She rolled her eyes. "Sure he is. Because you're totally dating, right?" She looked me up and down, her perfect tongue touching the corner of her mouth. "He'd never date a girl like you. You're not his type. That's why you're at this bar alone. Trying to pick up, huh?"

Jesus. "Butt out," I told her, narrowing my eyes. "Why are *you* here? Where's Josh?"

"I'm on a girls' night out. And I know exactly where Josh is," Gina said, putting a slight emphasis on my ex-boyfriend's name. "Josh is not your problem, honey. Nick is."

"What does that even mean?" I was angry and helpless at the same time, and I didn't know why. It was just the sight of her, when the last time—the only time—I'd seen her, she'd been half-naked after fucking my boyfriend.

"Josh told me about you," Gina said. "Little Miss Mommy's Girl. Practically picking out rings. You think Nick is going to fall for that?" She tutted. "He'll use you and dump you, if he even bothers. You're a total fucking bore, and you need to stop eating so much cheesecake. And I'm supposed to believe this little lie that he's fucking you?"

My mouth opened, and the words came out automatically,

like a bitch reflex. "He keeps his condoms in the top right drawer of his bathroom vanity," I said. "We used three of them last night."

Gina paused, her glossed lips parted as she stared at me.

"He likes blow jobs," I said. "A lot." This was an educated guess, because Nick. Also, every guy liked blow jobs a lot. "He likes it best when I swallow." Again, this was Nick—another educated guess. "Also, fuck you. Can I go now?"

She still looked at me, as if assessing whether I was lying, and suddenly I was so close to saying it: *Josh is cheating on you*. It was the truth, and I knew it, and she didn't. She wasn't so different from me. I could say those words and hurt her right now. I could ruin her snooty girls' night out with her snooty friends in her tiny red dress. I could tell her about Alison and Valentine's Day and all the things I knew.

And I didn't. It was partly because we were standing in a bar, with people walking by, and I had a complete revulsion for having this conversation here. But it also came from a second reason: I wasn't mean. I wanted to be. Right now, I wished I was. But I wasn't.

Gina's gaze flicked to something past my shoulder, and she licked the corner of her mouth again. It was probably a nervous tic of hers that men found unbearably sexy.

Someone came up behind me, and I smelled leather and laundry soap as a male chest pressed to my back. Nick's familiar hand came around my waist from behind, and instead of simply grabbing me, he played it just right: he slid his hand over my belly, his palm warm through the fabric of my dress, taking in my contours as he took his time, ending by cupping his fingers over my hipbone. At the same time he tugged me back so he was pressed flush against me, his hand angling me so my ass was pressed snugly against his hips. All of this right in front of Gina's surprised expression.

And just like that, my body woke up, my blood singing, every nerve ending alive. I didn't even have to look at him—just his hand, big and sculpted, pressing against my hip and the fabric of my dress, his arm clad in black leather, the two familiar bracelets on his wrist. I'd seen a hundred men tonight, and I'd met half a dozen, and the thought of a single one of them putting a hand on me like this made my stomach turn. And when this one man touched me, everything went nuts.

He dipped his head so his lips brushed the side of my neck. "You ready to go, babe?" he said in that awesome low voice of his, making my pussy throb with the vibration of it.

I put my hand over his. "Yes," I said.

He paused for a second, and I could tell he was reading me. The tension in my body, the rise and fall of my breath, my grip on his hand. He was reading exactly what I was feeling. Then he lowered his lips again and kissed the side of my neck—just a brief kiss, gentle and familiar, as if we did this all the time. He ignored my sweaty skin and my sticky hair and just kissed me.

And in that one, wild second, while he did that, I was absolutely fucking crazy about him. I would have done anything for him at all.

He lifted his head again, and I remembered Gina. She was standing there. This was all for her benefit. A good show, really. Maybe he wanted to make her jealous. Maybe that mattered to him. I didn't really know, did I?

Nick took a step back, pulling me with him. He turned toward the exit, his hip against mine, his arm still around me. He looked at Gina over his shoulder. "Excuse us while you go fuck yourself," he said, and led me away.

FOURTEEN

He kept his arm around me as we walked through the exit. He kept it there as we walked down the front steps to the sidewalk, then around the corner to the lot where he'd parked his car. He didn't say anything, and neither did I. I looked up at him and saw his profile was hard in the darkness, his jaw twitching.

"Thank you," I said.

"For what?" His voice was low and dangerous, a warning, though I didn't know what it was warning me of.

"For coming to get me. For doing that back there." I swallowed. "For making me look good, I guess."

We'd reached his car—a low-slung black thing that matched his black jacket and his black t-shirt and his fuck-you attitude. He turned me so my back was against the passenger door, and then he braced his arms on the car, boxing me in. "You think that's what that fucking was?" he said.

His eyes were dark as ink, unreadable. I didn't know what he was thinking, whether he was angry or turned on or disgusted.

Whether he thought I was a slut or a loser or just some girl he'd forget about an hour from now. We weren't compatible, and we'd been useful to each other and nothing else, but in that moment, I wanted to know what he thought of me. I wanted to break him open and look at all of his pieces, understand them—this one man, of all people. It mattered. I cared.

I shouldn't. But I did.

"Why did you come?" I challenged him. "It wasn't for appearances. You didn't know Gina was going to be there. So why? Why did you even call me tonight after you turned me down?"

"Jesus." He leaned closer, lifting a hand and digging it into the hair at the back of my head. "You're a fucking head trip, you know that? I don't know why I bother."

That stung. I could smell him, so close now. I was breathing his air, his heat, and I was taking deep breaths to take it in. "I take it back," I said, fighting it as hard as I could with every last part of me. Fighting and losing. "I'm not thanking you. You're an asshole, just like you said when I first met you. You don't care about anyone but yourself. You can go home now."

"Unfuckingbelievable," he said, the word soft under his breath as his big hand tightened in my hair. The pulse between my legs beat harder as I felt the pull on my scalp. "Are you done winding yourself up? Take a breath and come out of your head for one fucking second."

"Nick."

"Stop talking, Evie."

"I think—"

"Stop talking." He pressed against me, notching his hips between my legs as neatly as a puzzle, his jeans against my panties through my dress. I gave a little whimper of lust as I throbbed helplessly against him. He had me pinned to the car door now, his hand in my hair. I was immobilized, and instead of struggling, all I did was move my hips higher so I rubbed on him at just the right angle.

"Better," he said, so close now that his gorgeous mouth nearly brushed mine. "Much better. Do that again."

I hitched my hips like I was told, moving up and then down. I was so sensitized that I could feel everything—the rough denim of his jeans, the length of his hard cock behind it. He didn't move but braced against me, letting me rub him again, a demanding gesture. Me taking what I wanted. He was letting me do that, make demands on his cock, and I reveled in it, lightheaded.

He leaned closer and I felt him moan low in his throat, his breath against my neck. "So fucking good," he said.

"Nick," I breathed. I'd forgotten the bar and the parking lot and the rest of the world. My whole existence was his body against mine, his hand in my hair, his hips between my legs. My panties were wet where I rubbed against him.

He hissed in a breath, and it hit me that he was turned on, so fucking turned on he was holding on as tightly as I was. The thought gave me a rush of power, and I rubbed him higher, near the head of his cock behind his jeans.

His hand gripped my hair tighter in response. "Fuck, redhead, you fight dirty," he said against my skin. "You fight dirty, you get dirty. Is that what you want?"

Had I ever wanted anything else with him? I didn't think so. It was a relief just to say it. "Yes," I told him.

"Say it," he said, pressing his hips harder into mine, torturing me.

"I want it dirty," I said, the words a rush in my throat. "With you."

He pulled back. "All right," he said. "Open your mouth." And he kissed me.

That kiss was everything. Everything I wanted. He tasted good, and his mouth was warm and soft, and his stubble was harsh, and he opened my mouth and kissed me like he owned me, like there was no part of my body he didn't know. It was hot and somehow perfectly familiar, like the kiss he'd given me in the bar minutes ago. He kissed me like we'd already fucked. Like we fucked all the time. Like we'd just finished fucking, and were about to do it again.

And I kissed him back the same way. Like I already knew what he felt like inside me. Like I knew what set him off, made him crazy, made him come. Because in that moment, I did know. It was me.

This was always going to happen, I thought, the realization hitting me hard. From that first second I'd seen him standing over Josh, his fist clenched, this had always been in the cards. It didn't matter how much fighting we did.

He broke the kiss. "My place," he said against my mouth.

"Yes," I replied.

And just like that, we both gave in.

FIFTEEN

Nick

This was not me. I didn't know who this guy was, but he wasn't me.

I always played it a certain way with women. I was always in control. When you're the one who can take it or leave it, you're always the one in power.

Tonight, I wanted Evie. Very fucking bad.

If she didn't want my chivalry, she wasn't going to get it. She was going to get me instead.

We were silent on the drive to my place. Evie's jaw was tight, her cheeks flushed. She was wearing a sexy but classy black dress and Andrew's jacket, her hair down over her shoulders. I couldn't take her or leave her right now. Not tonight, and not Evie.

We didn't have a word for each other as she followed me into my penthouse. Scout was sleeping in her dog bed, but she got up and wagged her tail when we walked in. I shushed her and told her to go back to sleep, and she lay back down, tucking her nose under her tail and obeying. Then I turned to Evie, pressed her against the kitchen counter, and kissed her again.

We tangled—there was no other word for it. It was an argument almost as much as it was a kiss. She pushed my jacket off my shoulders and I dropped it to the floor. I yanked her jacket off of her. She kicked off her heels and jerked up the hem of my t-shirt. We shed clothes piece by piece, wrestling with each other as I walked her toward the bathroom.

"Where are we going?" she panted against my lip.

"Shower," I said.

We didn't even stumble. In a second we were in the bathroom as her dress dropped to the floor and she hooked her thumbs into the waist of my boxer briefs. Still kissing her, I banged open the shower door, leaned in, and turned on the water.

"Why are we showering?" she asked.

"Because you stink, redhead," I said. She smelled like Cintano's, like sugary alcohol and hair product and other men. I wanted all of that off of her. I wanted just her.

"God, you're a jerk," she said, and then she yelped in surprise, because I pushed her back into the shower, under the warm spray. She was still in her bra and panties—lacy and black, because she'd been planning to get laid, which made me lose control again—and I still had my boxer briefs. We got soaked, both of us, the cloth sticking to our skin.

She sputtered, pushing her wet hair back from her face, but before she could protest I pulled one cup of her lacy bra down, exposing her nipple. Water beaded on her skin, and I bent down and sucked it off.

I heard her intake of breath, and I pulled the other cup down and sucked the other nipple, which was as wet and juicy as the first one.

"Do that some more," she said, reaching behind her back and

unhooking the bra. Her voice was throaty and turned on, but I still had work to do. I wanted her to lose it the way I was losing it.

I tossed the bra to the shower floor and moved my mouth up her collarbone, the warm skin of her neck, as I cupped her tits in my hands. Fuck, they were just like I'd imagined. A perfect fit, spilling past the edges of my palms, their weight settling in my grip. I ran my thumbs over her nipples, pinching them gently.

She made a satisfying *aah* sound, and her hands skimmed over the wet skin of my back, sliding down to the waist of my boxer briefs again. She reached down and squeezed my ass where the soaked fabric clung to it, then she peeled the briefs off me. I let go of her tits and helped, stepping out of them where they joined her bra on the shower floor.

Her eyes got hazy as she took me in. That was good. I spent a lot of time at the boxing gym, and right now every second was paying off. I'd double my workouts if it made her keep looking at me like that.

I stepped forward and tilted her face to mine, kissing her, tangling with her some more under the hot water. Her hand traveled down and wrapped around my cock, squeezing it, exploring it between us. Her other arm wrapped around my neck so I held her upright.

She leaned in and licked my earlobe as she rubbed me. "Is this King Cock?" she said in a sexy voice in my ear.

I put my hand over hers and stroked, using her hand, sliding us both up to the tip and down again. "Don't say you're not impressed," I said.

"I'm supposed to be impressed?—*Oh*," she said as I pushed her back against the wall. I kept using her hand to stroke me, and then I used it to press my cock between her legs, where her soaked black lace panties still clung to her skin. Together, we rubbed the head of my cock against her, back and forth, just a scrap of fabric preventing me from shoving into her.

She was breathing hard, stroking me obediently, rubbing her pussy against me as I dragged my cock over the soaked fabric. I found her clit and pressed it with my thumb through the panties, and her hips moved against me, pressing me into her harder. She was getting lost now, her self-consciousness nowhere to be seen as she ground against me, her legs parted, her hand on my cock. She was nothing but a fire of need for me, which was good, because I was already there.

"God, Nick," she said as the water ran down her perfect tits and into her belly button. She pumped against me. "I'm going to—"

"Yeah," I said. "You are." I dropped my hand from hers and stood back. While she stared at me in surprise, I leaned over and shut the water off. I took her hand and pulled her out of the shower.

She followed. She was in the zone, so turned on she would have done anything I told her to. She'd finally let go of everything. I wanted her to see that. I wanted her to see herself.

So I moved her up against the bathroom counter, facing the mirror. Through the steam from the shower she looked soft, almost unbearably sexy—her hair wet and tousled, strands sticking to her cheek and her neck, her lips parted, her eyes heavy-lidded, her nipples hard. I put her hands flat against the counter and moved behind her, stroking her back, down her spine, her hips. Then I pulled the wet remains of the black lace panties slowly down her legs, letting my fingers drag with them, along her thigh, the back of her knee. I crouched and pulled them all the way down, stroking my palm over her calf, letting the fabric drop to the floor. I took a second to admire the view from this vantage point—specifically, Evie's hot, rounded ass—and then I stood again.

I grabbed a condom from my vanity drawer and put a hand on her hip, locking gazes with her in the mirror.

"Watch," I said.

SIXTEEN

Evie

Watch. As if I could look away. As if I could look anywhere else but at his gorgeous body, the tattoo on his shoulder, the whorls of hair on his chest and arrowing down his stomach. The way his forearm flexed when he put his hand on my hip. The bracelets on his wrist. The steam on the mirror made everything seem dreamlike, as if we were doing this in some alternate world. Right now, that world was the only place I wanted to be.

I had never had sex like this. I had never done anything like this. Sex in the bad old days was something I did for approval, which gave it a nasty, nauseating edge. Sex since then was always in a bed, usually in missionary, after a minimum of three dates. Because that was how you were supposed to do it. You weren't supposed to be soaking wet, bent over a bathroom counter, rising up on your toes while a very hot, very bad boy spread your legs apart. You weren't supposed to be bracing yourself on your hands, moaning as he slid his fingers in and out of you. You weren't supposed to give a cry of pleasure when he rolled on a condom and pushed his cock into you, pinning you to the counter.

But I did. I gripped the counter as he thrust inside me, then again, then again. It felt so good I was almost lightheaded. I wanted nothing more than for Nick to fuck me, however he wanted, as long as he wanted. I was about to get my wish.

He paused and, still inside me, he leaned forward, running his hands up my sides and cupping my breasts where they hung down above the countertop. "Look at yourself," he said.

I did. I looked like someone else, someone I didn't recognize. This woman's hair was dark and wet, her lips were parted, her head was thrown back. She had a man's hands cupping her tits as he fucked her, and she was loving it. She was pure sex, a goddess.

"More," I said.

He cupped my tits harder and thrust into me again, and I cried out. The tops of my thighs were digging into the edge of the counter, and I didn't care. It felt good. I arched my back to take him deeper, and he groaned softly as he felt me move. Then he braced a hand on my hip and fucked me harder while I nearly dissolved in the steamy air.

"Touch yourself, redhead," he said in my ear while he rocked my life and my whole fucking world. "Make yourself come."

I moved a shaky hand from the counter and slid it down in front of me, between my body and the counter. He paused, watching as I brushed my fingertips over my wet curls, then deeper, finding my clit. It throbbed under my touch and I groaned.

"Fuck," Nick said, his voice throaty with sex as he watched me. I stroked myself, tentatively at first, then with more confidence as the sensation built. It was exquisite, stroking my clit while his big, blunt cock was inside me. It made the sensation deeper, with a darker edge. I rolled my hips back against him, willing him to move.

He moved out and in again, slower this time, less harsh. It built into the sensation I was already giving myself. He came all the way out of my body and pushed slowly in again, making me feel everything, the way my pussy parted for him, the way I accommodated him. When he had settled inside me he backed out again, making me make a sound in my throat of turned-on frustration. He bent and kissed my neck, his stubble scraping my skin and making me shiver as he positioned the head against me again.

"I could do this all fucking night," he growled.

No. I couldn't take that. I didn't think I could take even a few more minutes without coming or crying or falling apart. He pushed inside me again, slow, watching me stroke myself. "You ready for more, Evie?" he said.

"There isn't more," I managed. I was close. So close. "There can't be."

But he slid his hand over my nipple, then down behind me as he stroked the cheek of my ass. "You know what I see right now?" he said, stroking me, stroking in and out of me in front of the steamy mirror. "I see a woman who likes to fuck. Who can't get enough of it. Who was born for it. Who wants to be fucked until she can't stand up anymore." His hand moved over my ass, his thumb moving between my cheeks. The feeling was strange and made my toes curl.

"Nick," I panted.

"You'll come," he said. "I promise."

My clit was throbbing hard beneath my fingertips, and his cock moved in and out of me, and he slid his thumb inside my ass. And *I didn't care.* It was filthy and unthinkable and completely shocking, and it didn't matter. I rocked back against him, taking it, taking every kind of pleasure I wanted, in every kind of way.

And I came. It was an orgasm unlike anything I'd felt before. It shook me and turned the world white and made me scream.

And instead of running from it I chased it, chased every last second of it while my body convulsed and Nick kept moving, faster now and harder, chasing his own pleasure. I gripped the counter against the assault of his big, strong body, and for a minute I was a vessel, taking it and waiting for him to come, and it was glorious.

Fucking glorious.

He came, his fingers leaving bruises on the skin of my hips. I felt every part of it. And I loved it.

That was how Nick Mason ruined me for other men.

SEVENTEEN

Nick

We dozed for a while, catching our breath on the bed in the dark. Then I heard the polite scratching that meant Scout needed attention. It figured, after a scene like that, my fucking dog needed to go out.

Reluctantly, I got up. Evie had pulled the sheet over her and didn't move; maybe she was asleep. I quietly put on underwear, a pair of jeans, a zip-up sweatshirt, and nothing else. I grabbed Scout's leash and took her down the elevator and outside.

It was late—one o'clock, maybe. There was no one around except for a couple of drunk guys walking past and a few taxis on the road. I stood while Scout did her thing and stared at nothing. I felt numb and oversensitized at the same time, my skin tingling. My brain kept looping backward, seeing Evie in that mirror, then shorting completely the fuck out.

It was like a hangover—a sex hangover. I'd never felt like this before. Sex was just something I did, like eating a hamburger or taking a cool shower after a hot workout. You felt the need to do it, you did it, and you pleased yourself. Like with any guy, my dick needed semi-regular attention, and as long as it got it, I didn't think about it.

I was thinking about it now.

I was thinking about Evie. I could still feel her, on my palms, on my cock. I wanted to go back upstairs and fuck her again, make her make all those sounds again. I also wanted to run, get on a plane and get the hell out of here. She was too close. She had stripped pieces off me, and she didn't even know it. She could see the things I didn't want her to see. She could push salt in my open wounds and make it hurt. If only she knew.

She's a woman, that's all. Man up, Mason, and go back in.

I had no idea what had happened. Who I'd been while I had her in that shower, against that vanity. I had no idea what came next. And I *always* knew what came next—ever since Andrew's accident, I'd rearranged my life to work that way.

Scout finished her business and sat on my shoe, ready to protect me from any dangers that came from the street. I scooped her up and carried her back inside while she tried to lick my face. I was still wrestling with her when I came in the door of my penthouse and saw that Evie was up.

She was wearing my t-shirt, which she must have picked up from the floor where we dropped it when she tore it off me. She had tied her hair back in a messy ponytail. And she had found the cereal in my cupboards, along with a bowl and some milk from the fridge.

Her brown eyes widened as I came through the door. "I'm starving," she said, like it was an embarrassing admission. "Is this okay?"

"Sure," I said. "Pour me one, too." I put Scout down and unclipped the leash from her collar.

Evie watched me as she took out another bowl. "I would never peg you as a Chihuahua owner."

"She's not my dog," I replied automatically. "She was Gina's, but Gina didn't want her anymore."

Evie banged the second bowl down on the counter a little harder than necessary. "That sounds about right," she said. Her voice was tight, and I remembered too late that it probably wasn't the best time to bring up the woman who'd fucked her last boyfriend. The woman who had also been saying something I couldn't hear—but was obviously very freaking bitchy—to Evie in the bar last night.

That had pissed me off, seeing that. It pissed me off again to see how tense Evie's face was right now. So far Bank Boy had been my prime target for revenge in this whole mess, but Gina had just bought her way onto the list. "You want to tell me what she said to you?" I asked Evie.

She didn't ask what I was talking about. "Insults, of course," she said, dumping some cereal into my bowl for me. "The girl kind."

"Girl insults," I said, sliding the bowl away from her and picking up the milk. "What does that mean, exactly?"

Her voice was harsh. "Why does it matter?"

"It fucking matters."

She looked at me for a second, and then looked away, blinking. "I'm dull and boring," she said. "That was the gist of it. The fat part was implied. Also, I'm lying about sleeping with you."

Oh, yes. There were going to be consequences to this. "You're not those things," I said, "and you are sleeping with me."

Evie must have caught something in my voice, because she stared at me for a minute, distracted. Thinking about that scene in the bathroom, like I was.

Fuck, what we'd done in the bathroom. That was the hottest, dirtiest sex I'd ever had. And if it was the last thing I did, I was going to convince Evie Bates to do it again. To do *me* again.

"Yeah, well," she said after a second, clearing her throat, "I was lying at the time, so I had to make some things up on the spot to sound convincing."

"Oh yeah?" I asked, digging in to my cereal. "Did you come up with something good?"

She reddened. "I told her—um, I told her you like blow jobs."

I put down my spoon and stared at her.

She looked flustered. "Never mind. It was just—"

"I do," I said.

She got distracted again. I knew the feeling, because I was staring at her mouth, thinking about blow jobs. Thinking about how good that would be. I wasn't thinking of running away now; those thoughts had gone. I was thinking about her licking me and cupping my balls and—

"I told her you like it when I swallow," Evie said.

There was dead silence in the room. We just stared at each other across my kitchen counter, and I wondered which of us would leap over it first. Probably me.

"Evie, I swear to fucking God," I said, giving her a warning.

She licked her lips nervously as I came around the counter, stalking her. The move didn't make her any less sexy. "We should probably change the subject," she said.

"Yeah?" I came closer, put my hands on her waist, moved them down to cup her ass. "You want to talk about how I just fucked you raw, and I plan to do it again?"

Her jaw went slack at that, she was so turned on. She unzipped my sweatshirt and ran her hand down my bare chest. "We should talk first," she said vaguely as she touched my pecs, my stomach.

I leaned in and kissed her neck. She smelled clean, overlaid with woman-sweat and sex. I slid my mouth over her skin, taking it in. "What do you want to talk about?" I asked.

"I don't know. Anything." Her hands skimmed up to my shoulders, pushing the sweatshirt off and belying her words. I dropped the shirt to the floor. "We should get to know each other."

"Sure," I said. I moved one hand to her front, pressing it between her legs and cupping her. She was bare, no panties, and I could feel her heat. "I already know a lot about you, though, Evie. A fuck of a lot."

"That—that isn't the same thing," she said, breathing shallow. "We should talk about other things, not just sex, and—oh, *fuck*." My finger pressed between the lips of her pussy, rubbing where she was wet for me. Her eyes half closed as she fought for control. "Nick, that isn't fair. My underwear was ruined in the shower."

"It wouldn't have made a difference." I circled her entrance, sliding my fingertip in, feeling her tighten around me. "I'd still do what I'm doing right now."

"Oh." She tilted her head back, and I watched her neck, the fall of her hair, in complete fascination. Jesus, this fucking woman. "Wait," she said weakly after a minute, putting a hand on my wrist.

I stopped moving. "Yeah?" I said. I was thinking about whether to make her come here or in the bedroom, with my cock inside her. I was leaning toward option two. My cock was hard as a hammer in my jeans, ready to start the dirty work.

Evie seemed to forcibly get herself together. "We should talk," she said. "I mean it." She pushed on my wrist, and I took my hand away. She closed her legs, looking regretful. "We should eat our cereal and get to know each other."

Somewhere deep in my lust-addled brain, a warning bell went off. I didn't talk to the women I had sex with. I didn't get to know them. That wasn't me. But I looked at Evie's face, flushed and nervous, and it didn't cross my mind to tell her no. If I told her no, she'd get dressed and leave, and there was no way I was letting that fucking happen.

So I picked up my bowl of cereal and walked over to the sofa.

"You're agreeing?" she called after me, like she couldn't quite believe it.

"Sure," I said. I put my bowl down on a side table and kicked my shoes off, unzipping my jeans.

"What are you doing?" She'd come closer now, carrying her own bowl. She sounded alarmed.

"Getting comfortable," I replied. "It's two o'clock in the morning." I looked at her as I hooked my thumbs in the waist of the jeans and pushed them down. "You just saw it all, redhead. There's nothing new. Relax."

I kicked my pants off, and her gaze slid down over me, her cheeks getting redder. "You, uh," she said. She nodded toward my crotch, speechless. "Um."

I looked down. I still had a boner in my boxer briefs, hard as a rock. Pretty impressive, though of course I'm biased. "Yeah, well, you were just talking about sucking me off and swallowing," I said reasonably. "Don't worry, it stays where it is. What did you want to talk about?"

"Nick," she said, exasperated and obviously turned on, "we can't talk properly with that."

"It'll go down in a minute." Painfully, but that was how it went sometimes. I sat on the sofa and put a throw pillow over it. I picked up my bowl again. "Better?"

She looked like she wanted to protest, like there was a catch, but finally she gave in, moving to the other end of the sofa with her own bowl. She grabbed the blanket from the sofa's back and put it over her lap so I wouldn't see her bare pussy beneath the hem of my shirt. That was us, two classy people with our crotches covered. They should send us an invite to Buckingham Palace.

We ate for a minute—I had worked up a nice post-sex appetite—and finally she said, "I have questions."

The alarm bell went off in my head again, but I ignored it. "Go ahead."

She looked around my penthouse. "You own this place?"

"Yes. Trust fund. I didn't earn it."

She looked surprised at my words, but for some reason it was important that she know. I didn't want her getting the wrong impression of me. "What do your parents do?" she asked.

"Invest other people's money, and skim pieces of it," I replied. "And, apparently, pay off their kids instead of raising them."

I sounded harsh again, but it was the truth.

"So you don't get along with them," Evie said.

"They hate me," I clarified. "They think I'm a disappointment and a waste of space." They weren't wrong, but it didn't mean they had a claim on any of my mental real estate. Not after they way they'd abandoned Andrew for the crime of getting into an accident and not being whole anymore. I really didn't care what they thought of me, but fuck with Andrew and as far as I'm concerned, you're done.

"Who's Andrew?" Evie asked.

I stared at her in surprise. It was like she'd read my mind. Or had I spoken aloud? I was pretty sure I hadn't. "How do you know about Andrew?" It came out hostile, but I couldn't help it.

She looked taken aback. "The jacket you lent me," she said. "It had a business card in the pocket. Andrew Mason, programmer."

Now the alarm bells were going off like crazy. I wanted to get on a plane and take off again. But I calmed myself. It was okay if she knew his name, after all. It was just a name. "Andrew is my brother," I admitted—more than I'd admitted to any other woman I'd been with, no matter what dirty things we did in bed, or how many times. I'd never even said Andrew's name to a single one of them.

Evie put down her cereal bowl, which she'd cleaned out. "And?" she prompted.

No. I had nothing else. Just saying his name had been like

wrenching a rib out of my chest, listening to it snap. "And nothing," I said.

"Do you get along with him?" she prodded.

The back of my neck was sweating. "We get along fine," I said. "Do I get to ask the questions now?"

She didn't look finished, but she said, "Okay."

"Did you just fuck me to get back at Bank Boy?"

She stared at me, her lips parted in shock.

I wasn't sure why I had asked that. Partly because of the Andrew questions—I needed to shut her down, regain control.

But part of me actually wanted to know the answer. Whether I was the nearest convenient dick for her. Whether she was slumming it for revenge.

Because if she was slumming it, I needed to know now. I didn't ask myself why.

"I don't see how that's possible," she said, her voice getting tight with anger. "He's not here to watch us. And he already thought we were—"

"Not literally," I said. "In your head. You know what I mean. Did you fuck me to get back at him in your head?"

She let out an exhale of breath, like I'd shoved her in the stomach. Her cheekbones were red again, anger and sex mixed together, and I felt my cock wake up again beneath the throw pillow. He'd gone to sleep when we talked about my family. "You have some nerve, asking me that," she said. "You told me to fuck someone the first night we met. You said it would make me feel better."

"And did it?"

That hurt her for a second—I hadn't meant it to, but it did. Her jaw went tight and her lip quivered. Then she said, "Nick, if you don't shut up I'm about to throw my cereal bowl at you."

Great. Now I was an asshole. Usually I didn't care, but this was Evie. "It's just a question," I said. "I want to know."

"You want to know?" she said, her voice getting higher, more wound up. "I don't know. I don't know *anything*. I don't fuck people, all right? I don't just do it. Some people do, but not me, not anymore. And I've had the worst week of my life, and you drive me completely crazy. What we did tonight—I've never done that. Not *ever*. Maybe it's routine to you, but it wasn't to me. It was something, but I don't know what, and I'll probably obsess about it for weeks while you forget about it tomorrow. That's it, all right? That's all I know."

She didn't think that was an answer, but it was. My mind stopped at those two words, *not anymore*. So she wasn't as square as she tried to be, redhead Evie. Just like I'd suspected. But whatever she'd done in the past, I didn't care. Not even a little.

I had my work cut out for me. I put down my bowl and tossed away the throw pillow. "You think that was routine?" I said, as her gaze dropped. "That's what you think?"

"I don't know what to think!" Her anger was mixed with lust now, and maybe a little fear. Not of me, but of herself. "I mean, you have a drawer full of condoms—and maybe you were trying to get back at—"

"Do not," I said, my voice a low warning. "Do not say that name. I do not want to fucking hear it ever again. Now, take that blanket off and open your legs."

She stared at me for a second. Shocked, flustered, affronted, turned on.

Then she did it.

I won.

EIGHTEEN

Evie

I wasn't going to give in. I was going to tell him to stuff it, and then I was going to get dressed and leave, go home and get on with my life without Nick fucking Mason. He deserved it.

Instead, I pulled the blanket off my lap and opened my legs.

Damn it.

I couldn't really blame myself. Nick without clothes on was a serious sight. All those muscles, that smooth skin. That bad boy tattoo. Those sexy hands, that sexy stomach. His cock was huge and hard for me—I had done that to him. He was leaned forward, prowling over the sofa toward me—there was no other word for it —and my body took over. My brain went stupid and shut up, because my body knew what that cock felt like now, and wanted it again. Again and again and again.

He put his hands on my hips and pulled me forward, scooting my butt down the sofa, making my t-shirt ride up so it showed my belly as I unbalanced backward. He grabbed the backs of my knees and pulled them apart and up, so my knees were bent below my armpits and I was completely exposed to him. I was panting, and I could feel how wet I was. He would be able to see it, smell it.

What had we been talking about again?

We'd been fighting about something. He'd made me mad about something. Now he was tracing the insides of my thighs, sliding his big hands up toward my pussy, brushing it with his fingers, and I wasn't mad anymore. All of the energy from the anger had turned into pulsing desire. I wanted to yell at him and I really, really wanted to come. Given the position I was in, I knew which impulse was about to get satisfied.

He hitched his body on the sofa, changing his position, moving his knees back, and then he bent and licked me, fearlessly, along my slit from bottom to top and down again, his tongue slick between my folds.

I let out a shaky breath and made a little mewling sound. He licked me again, going slow—testing, exploring. I could feel it. He was trying things. Figuring out exactly what made me crazy.

It worked. What made me crazy, it turned out, was when he licked down, then up, pressing my clit with the flat of his tongue. It turned out that made me completely fucking wild. I pressed my head back and fought for breath. Twisted my hands on the sofa arm above my head. Pushed my hips up into him. Kicked one of the empty cereal bowls off the coffee table, then tried to squeeze his head between my thighs. He didn't even care. Just pinned my legs open and kept going, doing exactly the right thing until I went to that place where I was so close... so close... the place where everything stopped, where the world went away and there was nothing except Nick's tongue, which was the best thing that had ever happened to me. I was, while he held me in that place, completely religious about that tongue.

And then I went over the edge. This orgasm shot up through me like lightning, cracking through my body in a hard flash that made me go silent in shock before I made more embarrassing sounds. A few hard twists and it was gone again, leaving me wrung out and unable to move.

Nick lifted his mouth from me at last. I could feel his breath between my legs. "Jesus, redhead," he said, his voice strangled and hot. "When you come, you don't fuck around."

I had no words to say. I lifted my head and looked at him, braced on his arms over me, his eyes ink-dark again. I had never seen anything so beautiful in my life. He took my breath away.

I pushed myself up on my elbows, then up. And then, struck by a perfect flash of inspiration, I slid down to the floor on my knees.

His eyes widened for a second when he saw my intent. He took me in, on my knees on the floor, taking in every detail of me. "You want to see if I really like blow jobs?" he asked.

"Yes," I said. "Please."

He pushed his boxer briefs off and sat up, his knees apart. I moved between them. He pulled his T-shirt over my head and off me, throwing it away as I raised my arms. It was like a practiced dance, neither of us speaking. Naked, I put my hands on his hot, muscled thighs and leaned forward, sucking his cock into my mouth.

He made a low, growly sound, very turned on and male, and the sound made me shiver. I braced myself on his legs and leaned in further, taking him deeper, sucking in the taste of him. He was big and very hard and utterly delicious. I moved my mouth down him, then up, taking him in the way he'd taken me in, exploring his skin, the head, my tongue moving over him. He pulsed in reaction in my mouth.

"Fuck," he said, trying to hold on.

I decided not to have mercy on him. He didn't deserve it. My position was perfect for what I wanted to do, so I did it. I gave him head that I hoped he'd never forget.

I took him deep, slowly at first, and then in a rhythm, over and over. I used my tongue on him, my lips. I'd given blow jobs before, but never like this. I was a genius, and Nick's cock was my area of expertise. In seconds, I knew everything I needed to know about it, every inch of it, every throb of reaction. When it came to Nick's cock, I was an artist.

I could feel his body tighten, his breathing get shallower. I wondered if he was watching me. He probably was. I pressed him deep into me, until the head of his cock hit the back of my throat, and I felt his hand twist softly in my hair. "Jesus Christ, Evie," he said in a tone of wonder and appreciation that made me wet again. "Jesus fucking Christ." I kept at it, relaxing my throat, feeling him thicken in my mouth. This was what he liked, then. Two could play this game.

Seconds later, I evened the score. He came hard in my mouth, his come in hot spurts in my throat as his body pressed up into mine. I swallowed, something I'd never done with any other man before. I'd said he liked it, after all. Time to find out if it was true.

When he'd finished I sat back on my heels, wiping my mouth. My mind spun, but I had no chance to put my thoughts together before Nick was on the floor too, on his knees, his hand on the back of my neck. He pressed my mouth to his, kissing me long and deep. Maybe he tasted the remnants of his own come; I had no idea, but the thought made me even hotter.

He broke the kiss, and without another word he put an arm around my waist, pulled me to standing, and flung me over his shoulder. I made an *oof* sound as he walked me into the bedroom and flung me down onto the bed. Still not speaking, he crawled over me, bracing himself on his arms and kissing me again. I was like hot liquid beneath him, beneath that body, that kiss, the wordless determination of it, like he couldn't stop himself.

He broke away again. "Ten minutes," he said, his voice

hoarse. "Give me ten fucking minutes, and I swear I'll fuck you again."

"Okay," I said against his mouth.

His mouth trailed down to my breast, my nipple. "You get anything you want," he said. "Think about it. Get creative."

I smiled in the dark. At least he was appreciative. "You really do like blow jobs," I said.

"That wasn't a blow job," he said, his scruff brushing my breast. "That was some kind of voodoo thing."

"I'll stick pins in you later," I said.

"Fine," he replied. "Just let me fuck you first."

AN HOUR LATER—BECAUSE he took that long to exact his revenge, which finally had me begging him—we were under the covers, tangled up and half asleep, when I remembered what we'd been fighting about. He'd asked me if I'd had sex with him to get back at Josh.

It had made me mad at the time, but now I wondered: Why had he thought that? Why did he think I wouldn't have slept with him otherwise? Did he ask me that just to piss me off? I hadn't missed the fact that he'd changed the topic when I asked about his brother. Maybe it had been a distraction question, though I didn't know why. Or maybe, in Nick's world, it was perfectly plausible that a woman would have the best sex of her life with a man, just to get back at somebody else.

He seemed so simple on the surface, but it was deceptive. There was something going on beneath that I couldn't see.

"Nick," I said.

He was lying on his side, facing away from me. I stared at his gorgeous, muscled back.

"Mmm," he said, his voice sleepy.

"Come to dinner," I said.

He rolled over onto his back, rubbed a hand over his face. I could see his tattoo, the bracelets on his wrist. The tattoo meant something, I was sure of it, and so did the bracelets. Something he wouldn't admit to.

"What?" he asked, confused.

"Come to dinner," I said again. "Tomorrow." I remembered it was the wee hours of the morning. "Today, I mean. At my mother's. Don't get leprosy or go to Mars. Come to dinner instead."

He frowned a little staring at the ceiling. "You don't want me there," he said. "You said it's a bad idea."

I had. I had said that. He should have told me off for saying that to him, that he was basically an embarrassment, but he hadn't. He seemed used to it. "It's just dinner," I said. "You should come." Too late, I remembered him saying he'd never met a woman's family. Maybe he'd laugh and say no way.

He just blinked and turned his head on the pillow, looking at me. His gaze took me in in the dark. I could see him thinking, could see something behind his eyes. I just didn't know what those thoughts were.

"You want me to?" he said at last.

"Yeah," I said. And I did. I didn't want to go to dinner by myself. I wanted him there.

He looked wary, and then he frowned in confusion again. This was really, honestly a situation he'd never been in. "Okay," he said finally.

I smiled a little. It was kind of cute, how being invited to dinner at my mother's house baffled him. I punched his shoulder. "Relax," I said. "It's roast chicken, not marriage."

"You're not making this sound super fun, Evie."

"You worried I'm going to domesticate you?" I teased him. "It'll be fine. You get to keep your balls, I promise."

"Still not selling it," he told me.

"But you're coming," I said.

"Sure," he replied. "I'm coming. Now get some sleep."

I closed my eyes. I liked Nick's bed; it was heavenly. My body was sore and warm and wildly satisfied. I had made, possibly, the worst decision ever. The man in bed with me had insulted me, driven me crazy, and fucked me six ways from Sunday. He'd put his cock in my mouth and his thumb in my ass, had said the filthiest things imaginable in my ear, had made me beg him to make me come. And I was taking him home to meet my mother.

I should be worried. Freaking out. Instead I was asleep in seconds, the best sleep I'd had in weeks.

NINETEEN

Nick

Evie's mother lived in a suburb that looked a lot like Andrew's, except on the other side of Millwood: modest bungalows, built decades ago but well kept. Except Andrew had picked his house because a one-story bungalow was best for a guy in a wheelchair. Evie's family owned a house here because it was what they could afford.

Evie drove us, since she knew the way. She went home first, washed and changed, and then she picked me up. She owned an old Tercel that had been repaired a lot but still ran. I'd never seen her car before.

"I think I should warn you about my mother," she said.

She was nervous again. She'd put on jeans and a sweater, her red hair up in a ponytail with strands coming loose. No makeup. Her hair gleamed in the sunlight. She looked pale, and it was only partly because we'd fucked each other to exhaustion last night. It was also because she was stressed.

"It'll be fine, redhead," I told her.

"About that," she said. "I'm not."

I looked at her. "What?"

"I'm not a redhead," she said, touching her ponytail self-consciously. "I think I should be honest."

"Evie, I have no idea what you're talking about."

"I dye it." She kept her eyes on the road, like this was a difficult confession. "I like the color, okay? I figure you should know." Her cheekbones went red in that telltale way. "You may have noticed, um, that the carpet doesn't match the drapes."

I would have laughed if she wasn't taking it so seriously. Also if she hadn't indirectly mentioned her pussy, which distracted me for a second. Then I remembered what we were talking about. "I didn't look at the color of the carpet," I said.

"Well, it's not the same. And you keep calling me that, so I thought—"

"You're a redhead," I told her.

"I just—"

"Jeez, Evie, is your hair red?" She shrugged. Christ, she was all wound up again. "Then you're a redhead. Now tell me why your mother freaks you out so much."

"She doesn't," she said, but it was a lame defense. She huffed a sigh. "I just think I should warn you. My mother is very conventional. Like, very. She's going to think that because you're having dinner, we're getting married and having babies."

"We're not," I said. "I'll deal. Anything else?"

"You don't get it," she said again. "My mother was educated by nuns."

It sounded like a figure of speech. "Literal nuns?" I asked.

"Literal nuns," Evie said. "She went to convent school until she was eighteen. She was going to actually become a nun, but then she met my father and decided she wanted to be a wife and mother instead. My father is the only man she's ever even looked at, as far as I know. And since he died when I was fifteen, it's just been her and me and my sister."

I hadn't even known her father was dead. "Fuck, Evie, I'm sorry."

She shook her head, but her expression was tight, because it hurt. I could see it. "He had a heart attack. We told him to quit smoking so many times." She shrugged, hard and sharp. "High school wasn't very good for me."

It clicked. I'd already figured out she had a past that included partying and sex, one she was trying desperately to leave behind. I had a hunch that past had started around the time her father died. I knew a little bit about how tragedy could fuck you up, derail you. But I didn't want her to start crying while we were still driving, so I changed the subject. "You have a sister?"

She nodded. "Trish. She's only seventeen. There was a big gap between me and her. Eight years, and she was only little when Dad died. I think maybe Trish was unexpected, you know? But I've never asked my mother about it, because of the nuns."

"Right," I said. "The nuns."

I'll admit it, the nuns were spooking me a little. I'd never met someone educated by nuns, and I'd pretty much debauched the woman's daughter. I wondered if I'd trail smoke and brimstone when I entered the house, like Temptus did in the cartoons Andrew and I made.

I'd been half asleep and orgasm-drunk when I made this promise to come to dinner. But I was in it now.

"My mother is very nice," Evie said, "don't get me wrong. She doesn't mean to judge. She just literally has the mentality of about 1955. She's never dated, and she only watches a little TV. She's had the same job as a receptionist in a doctor's office for fifteen years. She doesn't understand anything about what it means to be dating right now. It's like a foreign language."

It was weird, how tangled up she was over this. "So explain it to her," I said.

"No, no." She shook her head. We were pulling into the driveway of her mother's house. "I can't do that. I can't talk to her about condoms and one-night stands and sex. I don't know who'd die of embarrassment first, her or me."

"Okay," I said, backing off. There was something else under the surface, something she wasn't talking about. But it was too late now. We were here. And her mother was already opening the front door to welcome us, like she'd been waiting.

Mrs. Bates was in her mid-forties, and she was freaking small. Tiny. She weighed maybe a hundred and ten, a portion of that the pouf of her permed brown hair. An actual perm. She wore pleated tan pants and a golf shirt tucked in, with a slim brown belt. Her face was open and kind, but she dressed like a catalog from 1984.

"Come in, come in!" she said. She took both of my hands in hers when I came near, squeezing them. "You're Nick? Well, how lovely. I'm glad you've come to dinner."

The house was immaculate, every inch decorated. Bunches of flowers and dried flowers. Twee little sayings in frames. Paintings of ladybugs. Framed photos of Evie and another girl who was obviously her sister—school pictures, high school pictures. The house smelled like roast chicken and sunshine.

Jesus Christ, it was the *Twilight Zone*.

I had never been in a house like this. Andrew and I had been raised in a big, cold house, where there were staff and we weren't allowed to touch anything. I was wearing jeans, motorcycle boots, a long-sleeved black Henley. I was pretty sure I'd washed it recently and it had no holes, but I wouldn't bet money. I'd taken a shower, so I hoped I didn't smell like dirty sex. That was all I could say for myself.

I really did not belong here.

Evie's hand grasped my wrist, like she knew exactly what I was thinking. Which she probably did. Her fingers were cold, and I remembered how freaked out she was. Strangely, that made me calm down. It was just a house, a chicken dinner, and a hundred-and-ten-pound woman. I'd dealt with worse shit in my life. It was no big deal.

Mrs. Bates gave us cups of Perrier water—no alcohol, which was probably a blessing—and chattered on to Evie about inconsequential things as she bustled around the kitchen, getting the meal together. Then Mrs. Bates turned to me. "Nick," she said, "you have to tell me. How did you and Evie meet?"

I looked at Evie. Her gaze was panicked. I realized there was supposed to be a cute story, one that didn't involve the scene of me standing over Bank Boy's bloody face while Gina wailed, bare-assed. Still, it was the truth. I opened my mouth to say something, maybe leaving out the bare ass or the obvious fucking.

But Evie answered first. "Mutual friends introduced us, Mom," she said.

Mrs. Bates pulled out a salt shaker for the roast potatoes. "Like a blind date?" she said. "How nice."

"Like a blind date," Evie said.

"Well, it was a good choice, because you two hit it off so quickly," Mrs. Bates said, putting a slight emphasis on the last word. "What do you do for a living, Nick?"

Evie opened her mouth, but I was faster this time. "Nothing," I said.

Mrs. Bates' eyebrows went up. "Oh? You're between jobs?"

"No, I mean I don't do anything for a living."

Evie jumped in. "Nick is figuring out what he wants to do."

"Not really," I said. "I don't do anything. By choice."

Mrs. Bates watched us, looking back and forth. "I don't understand."

"I have a lot of money," I explained, "and I don't have to work. So I don't."

For a second, Mrs. Bates looked helpless, like I'd just told her I was from the planet Zorcon. Then she turned and looked at Evie. It was a strange look, full of meaning, and Evie's cheeks went red.

"Evie," Mrs. Bates said.

Evie crossed her arms over her chest. "What, Mom?"

Mrs. Bates sighed and seemed about to say something, but someone else came into the kitchen. She was curvy like Evie, her brown hair in a lumpy short braid over the back of her neck, and she wore a big sweatshirt that had a photo of Blondie on the front. She stopped in the doorway when she saw me.

"Hey, Trish," Evie said. "There you are. This is Nick."

I nodded at her, and she managed a faint "Hi."

"How is school?" Evie asked her.

"Whatever," Trish said. She pointed at me. "Evie, *this* is your new boyfriend?"

"Trish," Mrs. Bates chided. "Manners."

I was surprised for a second about the word *boyfriend*, though I supposed I should have expected it. "You got a problem?" I asked the little sister. "What's wrong with me?"

"You're totally good-looking," Trish said. "Evie usually dates dogs."

"Trish!" Mrs. Bates was shrill now.

Trish rolled her eyes. "That guy with the goatee?" she said. "Please. And Josh was just creepy. His teeth were so white."

Okay, I liked the little sister. But Evie rubbed a hand over her face. "Oh, my god. Can we eat now?"

I was still staring at the little sister. Trish. "What guy with a goatee?" I asked her.

"He was so *lame*," Trish said. "He worked in insurance, but he said he wanted to learn guitar in his spare time."

I looked at Evie. "For real? Jeez, redhead. Thank God I came along. Every guy before me was a warm-up."

"Nick," Evie said.

That was when Mrs. Bates banged the pan of chicken on the counter a little harder than necessary. "Time for dinner," she said. "Let's go."

TWENTY

Evie

Dinner did not improve things.

I was tense. I knew it. I knew it was out of proportion, and I knew it wasn't helping. But there was nothing I could do about it. Sitting here at the table, with Nick's crazy presence next to me, I felt ready to jump out of my skin.

Every guy before me was a warm-up.

I had brought guys home before, like Trish said. Josh, and before him the goatee guy (his name was Dave.) This should be no different. Except those guys were not Nick.

He was like a crackle of lightning, sitting next to me at the table. An insanely hot guy in a worn black Henley that showed the muscled lines of his shoulders beneath the fabric molded to his skin. I knew what all of that skin felt like against mine, what that sinful mouth felt like against mine, against the other parts of my body. I hadn't been a virgin when I brought the other guys home, but with Nick it felt like a neon sign: WE'RE FUCKING.

My mother was giving us disgruntled, uneasy looks. Trish just sat with her jaw open whenever she stared at him.

"Trish is trying out for the volleyball team next week," Mom said nervously, putting potatoes on her plate.

My little sister slumped in her chair. She was deep in the throes of teenage-girl derision these days, and in its annoying way it was kind of awesome. "I hate volleyball," she said.

"Tut," Mom said. "I'm sure you'll do fine." She turned to Nick. "Do you play a sport, Nick?"

Nick poked the chicken on his plate. "I box," he said. "I hit things."

"Oh," Mom said.

"I taught Evie to do it," Nick said. "She's pretty good."

Mom blinked in confusion. "You taught Evie to box? Is that safe?"

"It's no big deal, Mom," I said.

"It sounds fun," Trish said. "I'd rather box than play volleyball."

"You're playing volleyball," Mom said firmly. "It's respectable."

Trish went quiet, and I looked at her, feeling a chill of unease. Mom had said that to me plenty of times—*the job at the bank is respectable, college is respectable, that boy you're dating is respectable*. I hadn't thought anything of it. But hearing it said to Trish made me unhappy for some reason. "You don't have to be respectable," I told her.

"Yes, she does," Mom said, as if Trish weren't in the room. "She's in high school. It's a difficult time. I don't want her making bad decisions."

I heard my fork bang down on my plate before I realized I'd slammed it down. *Bad decisions.* I'd heard that one, too.

Next to me, Nick sat back in his chair and looked across the table at Trish. "What bad decisions are you gonna make?" he asked her.

Trish was sullen and glaring now, but her gaze went a little unfocused when she looked at Nick, like he'd hypnotized her. I knew the feeling. "I don't know," she mumbled. "Mom thinks I'm, like, going out every day and doing something stupid. And I don't."

I couldn't say anything, because that was my fault. I was the one who did stupid things, not her. My dinner went sour in my stomach.

"Trish," Mom said in her Mom-voice.

But Nick ignored all of us. "You flunk any classes?" he asked Trish.

Trish looked shocked. "No."

"Get detention?"

"No."

"Get in a fight?"

"No."

"You sound pretty good to me," Nick said.

"What is this?" Mom had put her fork down and was watching their exchange with worried eyes.

But I knew. I watched them and I knew. Nick was digging past the surface, because that was what Nick did. Somehow he knew what was going on, even though I'd never told him about Old Evie and the bad old days. I watched it like you watched a roller coaster that was about to go over the top part and down— like something you know you can't stop. Frightening and fascinating at the same time.

Nick picked up his unused dessert spoon and spun it over his fingers, then put it down again, the same gesture I'd seen in the diner the first night we met. "You ever get drunk?" he asked Trish.

"No," Trish said, but she looked uncomfortable. "Not really. Only a little."

"Trish!" Mom said.

"It was two wine coolers!" Trish nearly shouted back. "Jenny Cramer had them in her backpack! I'm seventeen, Mom. It isn't like I buy the weed that Peter Hadigan is selling."

"I'm sorry, what?" Mom sounded truly shocked now. "Someone is offering you *marijuana* at *school?*"

"I just told you I don't buy it!" Trish said.

"That's it." Mom picked up her napkin, then put it down again. "I'm putting you in a different school."

"Do you even know what year it is?" Trish was shouting now, all teenage drama.

I came out of my stupor. "Calm down," I told Trish. "Mom is just trying to look out for you."

"No," Trish said, turning to me. "She's just doesn't want me to be you."

There was dead silence at the table.

Then Nick's voice broke it with his low rumble. "What does that mean?"

I risked a glance at him. He was still sitting back in his chair, his dinner ignored. His posture was relaxed, but I could see the tension in it. He was looking straight at me.

"It means Evie was a bad kid." Trish filled him in. "I hear it all the time. *I had so much trouble with Evie. So much trouble.* She doesn't want me to be like that."

I locked gazes with Nick. His eyes were unreadable. I had a second where I was afraid he'd raise his eyebrows, needle me, tease me. Instead, he just looked at me, like he was seeing something new.

"You had a problem?" he asked. Just him and me.

"Evie sometimes makes bad decisions," Mom said.

I felt my face heat. Humiliation, anger—take your pick. I swallowed it down. "I got in trouble in high school," I said. "I almost flunked out. Then I, um, almost didn't go to college. Mom got me in. And I flunked that, too."

"There were parties and such," Mom said. "Or so I hear. You're impulsive sometimes."

I tore my gaze from Nick's and looked down at the table.

"I was worried to death," Mom went on. "You gave me a heart attack a million times when you came home late, or didn't come home at all. Then you left college, and I thought that you wouldn't have a career. You went to work at that bakery."

"I liked the bakery," I said.

"I never understood it," Mom said. "You were so difficult."

I slapped a palm on the table and leaned forward, looking at her. "I was difficult *because Dad died.*"

Another second of shocked silence. This was the worst idea I'd ever had, the worst dinner anyone had ever had. And I only had myself to blame.

Well, myself and Nick.

What must he think? That we were miserable and dysfunctional? Maybe he was right. We were. Besides, who was he to judge, when he didn't speak to his parents and refused to talk about his brother?

"Here's what I don't get," Nick said in the middle of the tension. "High school was a long time ago. Evie flunked out of college, what, five years ago? So what? That's a long time."

"The bakery was after that," Mom explained. "Thank God she got in at the bank."

I said the words. I could see the doom before my eyes, and still I said them. "I got fired from the bank."

"What?" Mom looked bewildered. "I don't understand."

Trish was looking at me with her mouth open in shock.

"Things were going so well," Mom said. "It doesn't make sense. You had Josh, and the bank, and now—"

"Hey," Nick cut in.

Mom went quiet, staring at him, pale-faced.

"I get it," he said to her. "You're doing the best you can. But when you talk to her like that, you make her feel like shit. So cut it out."

Oh, God. Oh, God.

"I beg your pardon," Mom said softly.

"You make her feel," Nick said again, more slowly as if my mother was hard of hearing, "like shit. Her little sister, too. Every time, you get it? Every time. So cut it out. If Evie wants to work in a bakery, she should work in a fucking bakery."

Mom pressed her lips together. "That's your idea of dinner table language?"

"It doesn't matter, since I'm not coming to dinner again," Nick said. "I'm one of Evie's bad decisions. We made a bunch of bad decisions last night. We'll make a lot more. And she's twenty-five, so it's none of your business."

"Oh, my God," Trish said. "Awesome."

"You," Nick said, turning to my little sister. "Stop being snotty. Don't try out for the volleyball team if you don't like it. And don't buy Peter Hadigan's dirt weed."

"I'm not snotty," Trish protested. "And how do you know it's dirt weed?"

"Because any guy who sells in a high school is a shitbag with dirt weed. Got it?"

"Can we please not discuss *marijuana* at the dinner table?" Mom said. She turned her glare on my so-called boyfriend. "You're right, Nick. You're not invited to dinner anymore. In fact, I think dinner is over. I'd like you to leave."

There was a second—just a split second—when I saw that she'd hurt him. But if you didn't know him as well as I did, you'd never see it. In a blink, it was gone.

"Got it," he said. He pushed his chair back politely and stood.

"Mom!" I said.

"He insulted me," Mom replied, "and he's giving your little sister advice about drugs. And he's swearing!"

Nick put a hand on my shoulder. "It's cool," he said. His don't-give-a-fuck tone was back. He didn't even seem angry. "You stay," he said. "Have a nice dinner." He left the room.

I stared at my mother. At Trish. At the empty doorway. Should I go storming out after him? Should I stay and let him go, let the situation defuse? I'd never been in this situation before, because this was the situation I'd always dreaded—bringing home a boyfriend who would upset Mom. My nightmare come to life.

And suddenly I realized I was twenty-five, and that was pathetic.

I turned to my mother. "I'll get him to apologize," I said, "but he's not wrong. You *do* make me feel bad."

"I don't know what you mean," Mom said.

"When you talk about what a failure I am," I said. "How impulsive I am. All of my *bad decisions*. That was a long time ago, and I've tried to do better, but it's never enough. I know you don't mean it, but it comes out like you're disappointed. Like you know that no matter what I do, deep down I'm still going to let you down." My throat choked closed, but I said the hardest part. "Like no matter what I do, I'm going to let Dad down."

Mom stared at me. Then she slumped a little in her chair. "Evie," she said.

"Because that's what it is, isn't it?" I said. "The reason I have to get a good job—the right job. The reason I have to date the right guy, and marry him, and have the right kids. None of it is to please you, not really. I don't measure up because I'm supposed to do all of it to please Dad."

"I don't—" Mom's breath hitched. "I don't mean it like that. It's just that if he were here... Evie, I've had to do all of it alone."

There were tears stinging my eyes. I looked at Trish and saw tears in hers, too. Well, this was the family dinner to end all family dinners. Welcome to my dysfunctional family. "You're not alone," I told Mom. "You have me. And Trish. And we both turned out pretty good. Dad is gone, Mom. We lost him."

Mom sniffed and wiped tears from her cheeks with her napkin. "You know I don't mean it," she said. "I don't mean—I love you both. He would love you both." She sighed. "Oh, my gosh, what a dinner this is. It's a disaster." She was right. The Nick effect, I thought. But Mom was a good person—the best person, really, deep down—and she straightened her spine and lifted her chin. "Okay," she said. "Go get Nick. I want to talk to him. We'll start over."

That was when I remembered that we'd come here in my car. Had he left? He didn't have a ride. I pushed my chair back and stood. "Shit," I said, swearing in front of my mother for the first time in my life. "I have to find him."

"Yeah, go find him," Trish said. "I like him."

I was already out the dining room door. He wasn't anywhere else in the house, so he must have left. I walked down the driveway, looked up and down the road. Nothing. My car was still there, the keys in my pocket.

Damn it, where did he go? Did he walk? Which way? Was he going to walk all the way home? I pictured him walking out the door and away, all alone. Kicked out of family dinner. He'd kind of deserved it, but that didn't make me like the picture any more.

I pulled out my phone and texted him. *Where are you?*

But half an hour later, when I got in my car and left after hugging my mother and my sister, he still hadn't answered.

TWENTY-ONE

Nick

I spent two days at the boxing gym, punching things.

That was the beauty of the boxing gym: you didn't have to be mad to punch things. You didn't have to have a cheating girlfriend or a shitty set of parents or a brother who got something he didn't deserve. You could be mad at those things, but you didn't have to. While you were punching the bag, you could only be mad at yourself. And the more you did it, the more numb you became.

So I went to the gym, and I punched things. The bag. Other guys, in the sparring ring. That had the benefit of me getting punched back, which suited my mood pretty well. Even with the safety guards and the gloves, it felt good to have someone hit me.

Evie texted me. I didn't answer her. I just went back to my life. I looked after Andrew, I looked after Scout, and I boxed. I got invited to parties like always, but I didn't go. I wasn't in the fucking mood.

It should have been fine. It was over anyway, me and Evie.

There was nothing to begin with. There never had been. It had always been just for show.

I had just finished my last punishing workout—the gym was closing, and they were kicking me out. I showered, changed, and had grabbed my bag when my phone rang. It was Andrew.

Andrew never called. When he communicated at all, he preferred texts—usually sentiments like *Pick up some coffee on your way over, dipshit* or *Where the fuck is the number for what's her face that comes on Wednesdays?* So when he called, I picked up right away. "What is it?" I said.

"Are you still in that shit mood?" my brother asked.

"Maybe."

"That means yes. Just call her, man."

I did not want to talk about Evie, and how I'd massively fucked everything up, so I said, "Did you just call to give me advice on my love life?"

"Aw, you have a love life," Andrew said. "How sweet. And no."

I hefted my bag on my shoulder and walked through the gym toward the door, which they were waiting to lock. Outside, the sun was setting. "So what is it?"

"I had a visitor today."

"Yeah? Who?"

"Mom."

I was dead silent. I let the gym door swing shut behind me.

"I know," Andrew said, as if I'd spoken.

I couldn't remember the last time our mother had visited either of us. When had she last been at Andrew's house? A year? More? "What the hell did she want?" I said, the words coming out harsh.

But Andrew didn't sound pissed. He sounded calm. "She came to tell me that Mom and Dad are getting a divorce."

I stood on the sidewalk on Norton Street, taking this in as the after-work crowd streamed past me. "What?"

"I know," Andrew said again, and fuck, it was good to have a brother in that moment, someone who understood. "I don't get it either. But she showed up on my doorstep today and said she wanted to talk. She said it's been coming for years, that she's been unhappy for a long time. She said she regrets how things have been, and she wants to change it from now on, now that they're split."

I started walking again. This was nuts. The thing was, our mother had always been useless, but she'd never been a liar that I knew of. Still, I couldn't help but be wary after all this time. "So it's all Dad's fault?" I said. "The fact that they haven't been around in years? Is that her story?"

"Not really. I mean, Dad is still checked out—he wants no part of this. But she didn't lay a big Dad rant on me, if that's what you're wondering. This was more about her and me. About us. I think she's been in therapy or something."

Andrew would know. He'd seen his share of therapists after the accident. He claimed it hadn't helped him, but he was blind to it. Or maybe he'd blocked it out. Because I remembered how bad it had been before he got help. I remembered perfectly clearly.

I had reached my car, and I opened the door and tossed my gym bag in. I found a baseball cap on the back seat, so I picked it up and put it on. "Fine," I said to Andrew. "So they split up. It was nice of her to drop by. But don't set your timer on seeing her again. She'll probably chicken out after this, just like she always does."

"She was sincere." Andrew's voice had softened in a way I had almost never heard it, and for some reason it made my heart twist painfully in my chest. Our parents' abandonment had hit him harder than he let on, and the tone I heard buried deep in his words had only one name: hope. After all this time, he was hoping Mom had changed, hoping she meant it, hoping this was going to work. After all this fucking time.

And that was good, right? That was supposed to be good? Why the hell did I feel like a black hole had opened up in the pavement below me and sucked me in?

Because it's supposed to be you he counts on. Only you, and no one else.

"Okay then," I said. I had to tread carefully with Andrew. I'd seen his mood tip in ways that terrified me, and I didn't want to set him off. Besides, he had enough shit in his life, and he didn't need an extra helping. If Mom bailed on him again, he'd still have me. "I hope it works out. I hope that now that she's dumped Dad, she can at least visit you every once in a while."

"And you," Andrew said.

I glossed over the fact that Mom's visit had left out her other son. I told myself it didn't matter. "Not likely," I said.

"It's likely. She wants to mend fences with you, too."

"Funny, I didn't hear my phone ring."

"Be serious, Nick."

"I am very fucking serious."

"Just do me one favor." Andrew's voice was on edge now, and I shut up. "If she wants to talk, just talk to her, okay? Listen to what she has to say. That's all I ask."

I can't, she'd said to me at the hospital that last time. *I can't, Nick. I just can't.*

I swallowed down my resentment and my hurt pride and all the other shit. "Okay," I managed. For Andrew. "If she shows up or she calls, then I promise."

"Good. You coming over later?"

Someone was coming around the corner of the gym to the parking lot. Someone with familiar red hair. I stood frozen in place. "What?" I said.

"Earth to Mason. You coming over later?"

She was coming closer. Her gaze was fixed on me, and she was walking fast. It looked like I was in big fucking trouble. "I gotta go."

"Oh, shit. Redhead alert?"

How did he know? "Something like that. See you later." I hung up and stood next to my car, waiting as she crossed the parking lot toward me. Her hair was down, blowing in the breeze. She was wearing jeans and a button-down shirt tied at the waist, over a white t-shirt. She looked ridiculously fucking sexy. I remembered what every curve felt like, exactly how she'd moved beneath me when I fucked her. Only this woman. Only Evie. I remembered every single fucking thing.

In boxing, it isn't always about hitting, it's about taking the hits, too. There's a certain way to take a hit so it minimizes damage. Your stance, the way you angle yourself so you're not unbalanced. So you can keep moving, take the hit, and hit back.

I just stood and faced her straight on. Sometimes you don't dodge, you take it. Even when it hurts.

"Hey," she said when she got close enough. "You haven't answered my texts."

"Evie," I said.

"Don't *Evie* me. I have been texting you. I texted"—she shoved me in the chest, hard—"you."

"Yeah," I said. "You did."

"See, Nick, this is how civilized people behave. Civilized people who are not assholes"—she shoved me again—"and who feel bad about wrecking someone's family dinner, then taking off without a word. Civilized people, when they get a text after that, they answer it. Preferably with the word *Sorry*."

I lifted my ball cap, scratched my forehead, then put the cap on again. "I got kicked out of dinner. I didn't take off."

"You did!" She was mad. Really mad. Why was it that Evie

Bates was only really mad around me? "Where the hell did you go, anyway? I looked for you. Do you have some secret transporter or something?"

"I walked," I said. "Part of the way, anyway. When I got tired, I called a cab. With my cell phone. No transporter."

"It was a figure of speech! I couldn't find you. You just left!"

"Because I was told to leave, remember?"

"Damn it, Nick. You couldn't just be *nice!*" She raised her hands to shove me again, but I was quicker this time. I grabbed one of her hands and pinned it behind her back, firmly but gently.

"I'm not nice," I said, leaning in close to her ear, smelling her hair and her skin and all the other things I remembered. "I've never been nice. I will never be nice. You knew that from the beginning. In fact, that's why I was useful to you in the first place."

She went still in my grip. From my position, my mouth just below her ear, I could see straight down into the cleavage of her t-shirt. She was mostly covered, but my imagination didn't need much to go on. I could see the beginning of the shadow between her breasts, and it made me want to pull every stitch of clothing off her. That was how not nice I was.

"I didn't mean it like that," she said.

"You meant it exactly like that." I had my arm around her waist, pinning her hand up against her back, and now I pulled her forward, pressed her slowly to me. I raised my head so my lips were an inch from her jawline, her cheek, the corner of her mouth. "You wanted a guy who isn't nice, well, you got him. That's me. I did you a favor, not answering you. You don't like it, go find Bank Boy's fucking twin."

Evie inhaled a breath. She was relaxing a little against me, some of the fury leaving her expression. She didn't try to get out of my grip. "So that's it?" she said, her voice not quite as harsh. "You just get to act like an ass whenever you want?"

"No," I said, meaning it. "I'll apologize to your mother. I disrespected her. Your sister too. But I don't promise I'm going to be nicer to them than I was at dinner. I don't promise to be fake and friendly. I don't promise to be tame."

"Damn it," she said under her breath, almost to herself. Her breath was mixing with mine, her mouth was so close to me. "Why are you like this?"

"What can I say? I'm complicated."

"You're a disaster," she said. She briefly bit her lip. "And you never taught me how to get out of this hold."

"We're face to face, Evie," I said. "Easiest way is to knee me in the balls."

Her eyes flashed like I'd given her an idea, but I let her go before she could act on it. I dropped her wrist, raised my hands, cupped her jaw, and kissed her.

She kissed me back. Slowly at first. Then she fell into it, just like I did, her mouth opening under mine, her body leaning in, her tongue tasting me. And it was all there. Her and me, everything there was, everything we'd done, it was right there between us. That kiss was the way we talked and the way we fought and the way we fucked. I kissed her and I could taste the way she came, on my cock or my hands or my tongue. I could taste the way she'd gone on her knees and sucked me off. I could feel everything. It was the only fucking thing I wanted anymore. And there was nothing I could do.

We broke the kiss, and she pressed her hands against my shoulders, curling them into fists. "Shit," she said. She punched my shoulder softly, with no bite to it. "Shit."

"Come back to my place and fuck me," I said, because that was what I wanted. And a man's gotta try.

She looked tempted, and she licked her lip quickly like she

could still taste me, but her spine straightened under my hands. "No," she said. "We're not doing that right now. I'm still mad."

"Angry fucking is the best fucking," I said. At least, it would be with her. An angry fuck with Evie would be like a volcano going off. But she backed out of my grip—reluctantly, I thought—and I let her go.

I watched her straighten up, focus. She crossed her arms over her chest and looked at me. "There's something I want from you first," she said.

I racked my lust-addled brain for a second. What could she want? She'd turned down sex. She wasn't the kind to ask for money. Aside from those two things, no one ever wanted anything from me. "What is it?" I said.

She reached into the back pocket of her sexy jeans and pulled something out. A small white square. A business card. "I want to know all about Andrew Mason, PHP programmer."

Shit. The business card she'd found in Andrew's jacket. "No," I said, the word automatic.

"Yes," Evie shot back. "You fucked up my family dinner. You practically just admitted it."

"I do admit it," I said.

"So we agree. And you saw my screwed-up family, warts and all. What I want in return is the same thing from you."

I shook my head. Andrew was off limits; Andrew was always off limits. "No way," I said. "No deal. My brother is nobody's business."

"Why? I assume he's a grown man who doesn't let you make all his decisions."

"Because he just is. All right? He just is."

She seemed to think it over. "Not good enough," she said. She held up the card again. "Either you take me to meet him, and show me whatever it is you're hiding, or I'll call him myself."

Damn it, she was fighting dirty again. "You wouldn't."

"I would." She put the card in her back pocket again. "I have his number. His email, too. I'll just introduce myself. Should I say I'm your girlfriend? Yes, I think I will."

She had me, damn it. Because I had no doubt she would do it. I felt cold sweat on the back of my neck. Why it was so terrifying, I couldn't really say. I just knew it was. "You sure you don't want to go fuck instead?" I asked in a last-ditch effort.

She gave me a little smile at that. A Mona Lisa smile. I could have jumped her for that smile alone. "Do this and I'm all yours," she said.

I groaned. Did I say she fought dirty? She fought fucking dirty. I reached behind me and opened my passenger door. "Fine," I said. "I'll do it. Get in."

TWENTY-TWO

Evie

We drove for a while in silence, and when we got to the edge of the suburbs, Nick pulled in to the parking lot of a strip mall and took out his phone. "I have to text him," he said. "Andrew doesn't like surprises."

He flipped through his phone, keyed a few words. Fuck, he was good-looking. It was ridiculous. Wearing one of his worn t-shirts, this one dark green, a black ball cap on his head, pulled down halfway over his eyes. Jeans with a hole in one knee. When he bent to his phone, I could only see the scruff of his jaw and his beautiful mouth. I wanted to lick the taut skin of his forearm and then jump him, hard. *Come back to my place and fuck me.* What kind of black magic words were those? Because I almost did it. He had no idea how close I came. How close I still was.

He waited a second, rubbing his lower lip absently while my insides clenched, watching him. *Be strong, Evie.* Right. There was no point in just going back to his place and fucking his brains out all afternoon. That would be counterproductive. Right?

The phone bonged a reply, and Nick put it down. "All right," he said. "He wants to meet you. He says we can come."

I felt a little nervous at that. Were we meeting the Pope? For the first time, it occurred to me that Nick's brother might have something wrong with him. Maybe he was sick. Maybe he had intellectual problems, or physical ones. Maybe he was mentally ill. In short, maybe Nick had good reason for keeping strangers away, and I was only intruding by insisting I had a right to barge in.

But it was too late now, and besides, Nick had agreed—and so had Andrew. So I sat quiet while he drove the rest of the way, through a suburb that looked a lot like Mom's. "Is there anything I should know?" I asked finally.

"Sure," Nick said. "He's grumpy and sort of an asshole."

"So he's like you then, except you're totally an asshole."

He grunted. "You'll see."

We pulled into a driveway, and I saw the telltale ramp that led up to the porch instead of stairs. Oh, shit. Maybe I was the asshole here.

"My mother isn't mad at you anymore," I said when he put his hand on the door handle.

Nick looked at me. "What?"

"After you left, I told her that you were a jerk, but you were right. She does make me feel bad. Trish, too. We had it out. She ended up listening. We've talked on the phone a few times." I shrugged. "Things are going to be okay, I think."

His gaze on me was hard. "Why are you telling me this?"

"I thought you should know. That's why I was texting you." I put my hand on my own door handle. "Let's go."

He led me to the porch, where he waved at a security camera and there was a buzz in response. He opened the front door and brought me in to a house like a million others, except not. Where the living room should be was a room full of computers and screens, and in the middle of it was Nick's brother.

I was surprised again. The ramp had made me think I was going to see someone helpless and sick, but that was an assumption. A stupid, clueless one. Andrew Mason was in a wheelchair, but he was good-looking and vital and strong. He had turned his chair to face the living room doorway so he could watch us come in. He was wearing a faded Hornets sweatshirt, so worn it could have come from Nick's own wardrobe, and jeans, with socks on his feet. His hands were folded in his lap, the fingers interlaced, as if he was making an attempt to look polite.

But it was his face that struck me. He was Nick's mirror image, except he was thinner and probably a few years older. His hair slightly darker, his jaw clean-shaven. But no one with eyes could mistake them for anything but brothers. It was like looking at Nick if his life had been different. I stood frozen for a second, shocked at the resemblance.

Then Andrew smiled, a wide smile I'd never seen on Nick, and he looked like a different person. "It's the redhead!" he said.

I blinked.

"Oh, shit," Nick said behind my shoulder. "Here we go."

"The redhead?" I asked.

Andrew unlaced his hands and held one out. "Andrew Mason," he said. "Nick's older brother and possibly his greatest nemesis. Nice to meet you."

"Evie Bates," I said, shaking his hand. His was big and impossibly strong. "Nice to meet you, too. I'm really sorry to interrupt."

"Interrupt what?" Andrew looked around. "I'm not doing anything. Fucking around on the computer, like I always do. I think"—he pressed his hands together, like prayer, then pressed his fingertips against his chin thoughtfully—"yes. I think you are the best-looking woman who has ever entered this house. Donna who helps me on Thursdays is an attractive lady, but she's been married for twenty-five years and she always wears Crocs. You have her beat on footwear alone."

I didn't know if he was joking, or if I was supposed to laugh, so I said, "Thanks."

"Shit, have a seat," Andrew said, turning in his chair and pushing a pile of papers and debris off an old sofa. "Do you want coffee? Nick will make you coffee."

"No coffee," I said, lowering myself onto the sofa, which had clothes and a pair of old sneakers still piled onto the other half. This was definitely the den of a guy who lived alone. Nick's condo was tidier than this, but not much. The similarities between the two brothers was amazing. "I'm fine."

"Well, I want coffee." Andrew looked at Nick. "Nick, make coffee."

"Be nice, fuckwad," Nick replied. "I didn't bring her here for you to scare the shit out of her."

"Evie looks fine to me, dipshit," Andrew replied. The insults weren't sharp, but were spoken like everyday language. "Go make coffee or something."

"Go fuck yourself," Nick said, and left the room.

It was weird. It was kind of funny, yet the tension was as thick as a steak. There was love between these two brothers, and insults, and something else unspoken. Something in the history between them that I didn't know. Something that had to do with me, yet had nothing to do with me at all. I couldn't make sense of it. But Andrew had obviously sent Nick out of the room for a reason, so I waited to see what it was.

When Nick had gone, Andrew pressed his hands together again, pressing his fingertips to his chin. His expression softened, and it was only when I saw it that I realized his expression had been tense in the first place. When he spoke his voice was lowered, quiet and sincere. "He talks about you," he said. "You're the only woman he's ever talked about."

I sat up straight, my stomach flipping. "What?" I nearly whispered it, like we were keeping a secret.

"He's never brought a girl here before," Andrew said. "Never." He sat back in his chair. "Let me guess. He hasn't told you anything about me?"

I shook my head.

Andrew let his voice fall back into normal range, so Nick could probably hear it. "I'll tell you what happened to me," he said, "since you're probably wondering. People always do, though they're too polite to ask. It's why I don't leave the house very much. I could, but what's the point?"

"You don't have to tell me anything," I said to him. "It's none of my business."

"I disagree," Andrew said. There was a bang from the kitchen, and Nick swore. Andrew flicked his gaze to the doorway, and for a second his look was fond and exasperated and so full of love I nearly got up and kissed him. Then he looked back at me and said, "I was in an accident five years ago. I was at a party, drunk. One of my buddies offered me a ride home. He was as drunk as I was, but I got in anyway." He shrugged. "The rest is history."

"I'm so sorry," I said. Then I winced. "Do I sound like a jerk? I sound like a jerk."

"You sound fine," Andrew said. "It's shitty. But my buddy died, and I didn't. So technically I got the better deal." Behind my shoulder, Nick came back into the room, and Andrew's gaze flicked to him again before he looked back at me. "I'll tell you the other thing people always wonder," he said, "since you're practically family and all. I can't walk, but the equipment works, if you know what I mean."

Nick banged the mug down on the desk next to Andrew, then sat on the sofa next to me. "Welcome to my world," he said. "You see why I didn't bring you before?"

"Just being honest," Andrew said, a glint of humor in his eye. It was dizzying, watching the Mason brothers piss each other off. Nick sat with five inches between us, not touching me, his whole body stiff with tension, like someone had buzzed him with an electric shock. I'd never seen him like this before. I'd never known he *could* be like this. And I realized I was seeing a side of Nick Mason, of his life, that no other woman had ever seen, if Andrew was to be believed. It wasn't Andrew that Nick had been hiding from me all this time, hiding from everyone he met. It was Nick himself. Who he was here. What this meant to him.

There was only me to see it. Only me. And I didn't know what that meant.

"Okay, we got that out of the way," Andrew said. "Evie, I hear you work in a bank. No, wait—you almost got fired from the bank. Right?"

"That's true," I said. Funny, since that night at my mother's I didn't feel embarrassed about it anymore. Especially with these two. "I'm pretty much fired, because I threw a mug of tea at my ex-boyfriend when he said I was dressed like a slut."

Andrew took a second to close his eyes in happiness. "That story gives me total joy," he said. "I like any woman who can whip a mug at a man's head. Go on."

"There isn't much else to say," I said. "Except that I'm not going back."

Andrew opened his eyes again, and I could feel Nick looking at me, too. "No?" Andrew said.

"No." I hadn't even thought it, hadn't formed the words in my mind, but when I said them I felt the truth of them. I wasn't going back there, to work with those people. To work with Josh. I decided right there on Andrew's ratty sofa. I'd rather do nothing, and starve, than go back there.

Except maybe I wouldn't do nothing. I had the beginning of an idea.

"Okay," Andrew said. "You're not going back to the stupid job where you have to work with the ex-boyfriend who screwed what's-her-name. That sounds legit. Jobs are overrated anyway. I have plenty of money, and so does Nick. We can help you out if you need it. Just say the word."

I looked at Nick. He was watching me, but I couldn't read his expression. "Sure," he said. "Don't sweat it, Evie. The rent's paid for as long as you want."

I had that knee-jerk reaction: *No way, I don't need any help, I'll be fine.* But my savings weren't endless, and no way was I going to Mom for money after I flunked out of college. So I said, "Thanks for the offer. I'll be okay for a little while, I think." Besides, if what I was thinking worked out, I might be able to figure it out. I wanted to try.

I wanted to try doing things the way I wanted for once. Living my life the way I wanted. I was only beginning to figure out what that was.

"I hate my job, too," Andrew said, sipping his coffee. "I'm a programmer. Freelance."

"I know," I said. "I found your business card in the pocket of a jacket I borrowed from Nick."

Andrew's eyebrows went up. "What jacket?"

"A jean jacket," I said.

"So that's where that went."

"She's keeping it," Nick said. "You're not getting it back."

I opened my mouth to protest, but Andrew said, "You're right, she should keep it. Evie, it's yours. It probably looks hot on you."

I shrugged. "I was wearing it when I got called a slut."

Andrew laughed, a real belly laugh that echoed around the room. Beside me, I felt Nick relax, his body practically transmitting to mine through the old sofa cushions.

"I never pictured it," Andrew said, his laugh winding down,

"someone getting called a slut while wearing that jacket. I think that means I have good taste in clothes."

"It doesn't," Nick said.

Andrew shook his head at him. "You're just jealous because no one called *you* a slut. Anyway, I'm a good programmer, but it's fucking boring. The other thing I'm good at is illustration."

Nick went tense beside me again. There were so many undercurrents to this conversation, I was starting to feel exhausted. "Andrew," he said in a low voice, "don't. Fucking don't."

I looked from one brother to the other. Maybe Andrew illustrated something disgusting or violent. Or porn. "I'm not sure I want to know," I said.

"It's not what you think," Andrew said, catching the meaning of my worry. "It's comics. They're great. Good stories, great characters. It started as a hobby after my accident, but you know what? Lately I've been thinking I really like it. Like, a lot. I want to spend more of my time doing it instead of just a hobby. I've been thinking I could really make something if I committed myself, you know? Create something that matters. I think that would be worth it."

Nick sat back on the sofa and rubbed his hands over his face. "Jesus, please don't," he said.

"Don't worry about my brother," Andrew said. "He'll be fine. I can show you. Want to see?"

Again I looked from one brother to the other. "You guys are making me crazy," I said frankly. "What's going on?"

Nick dropped his hands. "What's going on is that Andrew is going to show you his comics," he said, his voice resigned. "Apparently."

"What's the matter?" I asked him. "Are they terrible?"

"The drawings are great," Nick said. "The stories are terrible."

"The stories are *not* terrible," Andrew insisted. He had turned to one of his computers and was clicking. The screen behind his shoulder, facing me, woke up.

"They are," Nick insisted, which I thought was a little rude. He didn't have to insult his brother's creative work, after all. "It's like an amateur wrote them. An amateur in kindergarten."

"Amateurs in kindergarten can write great things," Andrew said calmly, flipping through some files on the desktop. "Especially if they believe in themselves."

I was going to ask another question, or maybe tell Nick he was being a jerk, when Andrew clicked an icon and a comic showed up on the screen. It was four panels, two on top and two on the bottom. The illustrations were awesome—some kind of devil-type man, with smoke trailing from his nostrils, holding a planet in the palm of his hand and grinning evilly at it. "My great experiment finally worked," the character said in the panel. "I've split the atoms in tiny planet Pluto. Now the entire planet is a live nuclear bomb!"

I got up from the sofa and walked to the screen, getting closer to read on.

The next panel featured a pretty girl with dark-framed glasses staring at a laptop. "Lightning Man," she said. "Get over here! The readouts I'm getting from outer space are strange. The radiation levels are changing by the second. Something weird is going on!"

The third panel showed a man leaning over the girl's shoulder. He had longish hair, brushed back from his forehead and tucked behind his ears. Slashes of brows and a sharp chin. He was wearing all black, the effect a little sinister and very cool. Apparently, he was Lightning Man. "You're right," he said to the girl in glasses. "It is unusual. And I think I know what it is..."

"You like it?"

I turned. Andrew was watching me read, his hands laced in

his lap again. He was grinning. Behind him, Nick sat on the sofa, his arms crossed over his chest.

"It's awesome," I said to Andrew. "You made this? It looks amazing." It did. It was cool and creative and beautifully drawn. "How much have you written?"

"Good question. Let me think." Andrew twisted in his chair and looked over his shoulder at his brother. "How much did you write, Nick?"

I stared at Nick, who looked uncomfortable.

"You wrote this?" I asked him.

He didn't meet my eyes, and then he did. He looked right at me. "Six volumes," he said. "Ten issues per volume. So sixty issues of Lightning Man so far, give or take."

"Give or take," Andrew agreed. "He writes them, I draw them."

This was amazing. I couldn't take it in. "Do you publish them?"

"You're looking at it," Andrew said. "This folder on my desktop. That's where Lightning Man is published. That's it." He looked thoughtful. "In fact, you're our first reader. Ever."

"But this is crazy," I said. "You should publish them or something. Put them online."

Andrew looked at Nick again. "See, I told you. She agrees with me."

"No," Nick said. "No fucking way."

I was still staring at him, trying to process the fact that Nick wrote comics, and apparently had been for years. "Why not?"

"I told you, the stories are no good. You think I know how to write a fucking story? I don't."

"I like them," Andrew said. "I'm *still* waiting for you to get Lightning Man and Judy Gravity together. I mean, you know it's gonna happen. It's just a matter of when."

"They have to dismantle the nuke in Pluto first," Nick said.

"And it doesn't matter, because no one is ever going to read them."

"Nick," Andrew said, "if we put them out there, *so many* people would read them. That's what I'm saying. And I think I want that. This is my work, too. I don't want it just sitting on my desktop anymore. I want it to go further."

"You could find a way to print them," I said. Because despite Nick's misgivings, this was amazing and exciting. "Sell print copies online. And you could publish it online, too, maybe as a subscription or something. Or sell downloads of the issues. People can read comics on their tablets."

"I can do all of that," Andrew said. "I could do a Lightning Man site in a couple of days."

"I don't get a say?" Nick said.

We looked at him. He was still on the sofa, rigid. "What is it?" I asked him. "This could be great."

Nick looked at me. "It isn't going to be great," he said, and his voice was icy calm. "It's never going to be great, do you understand? It's never going to be a success, because I wrote it. And I am not a fucking writer. I'm a dropout loser who does nothing but party, remember? That's what I am, and it's all I'll ever be."

I opened my mouth to argue, but Andrew spoke first. "We're doing it," he said.

I looked at Andrew. He was pale, with anger and hurt and something deep and dark under the surface that I couldn't read. He was staring at Nick, unmoving, his voice so flat it was scary. "We're doing it," he said again, the slightest tremor in his voice.

Nick stood up. "I'm going," he said, his voice thick, and he turned and left the room.

I looked at Andrew again, but he didn't even look at me. He stared at the empty doorway. Finally, he spoke. "You should go with him," he said, his voice an ache. "Sorry about this, Evie. We're a fucked-up family."

I stood up, reluctantly. "I have a fucked-up family, too," I said. "Are you going to be okay?"

He turned his chair so he was facing his keyboard again. "I'll be fine," he said. "Just go."

There was nothing else for me to do, so I walked out. And I left him sitting there, alone.

TWENTY-THREE

Evie

Nick was getting in his car in the driveway in the dusk. I wanted to think that he wouldn't have driven away without me, but in his mood I couldn't be sure. Maybe I'd end up walking home alone, like he had from my house. Two equally messed-up family meetings. What a pair we were.

Why had I ever thought this would work? *Had* I thought this would work? Everything in my life since Nick walked in was so confusing, so overwhelming, that I didn't know anymore.

I got in the passenger side. One thing I knew for sure was that he wasn't going to get away with being broody and silent. "Are you going to tell me what that was back there?" I said as he started the car and pulled out. "Because I sure as hell couldn't figure it out."

"There's nothing to say," Nick said. His jaw was tight, his eyes fixed on the road. I couldn't see all of his expression beneath the brim of his baseball cap. But I could see his knuckles white on the wheel, the tendons in his arm flexed hard as stone. I wanted to punch him and kiss him and drag everything out of him all at once.

But the one thing I didn't want to do was run. He didn't scare me, not even a little.

"There's plenty to say," I said. "That wasn't just an argument back there. That was something deep." I waited, but he was still silent. "Talk to me, Nick."

He wasn't taking me back to the gym, where my car was. He was taking me further out of town. Soon we passed through farmland, where handmade signs advertised apples and pumpkins and firewood. He took a right turn and I realized where we were going. "You're driving to Newcastle Point."

"You been there?" Nick asked.

I snorted. "Everyone who went to high school around here has been there at one time or another." Newcastle Point was secluded, it was nice, and it wasn't far out of town. In other words, the perfect spot for drinking, making out, and fucking if you got lucky. Old Evie had been to Newcastle Point a lot, but not since prom night.

"Let me guess," I said as he wound further down the road that led down the point. I could see glimpses of the lake through the trees, turning dark as ink as the last of the sun disappeared. "You never bothered with Newcastle Point in high school. You just screwed girls in your car, or up against a locker somewhere."

"You have a weird idea of my sex life," Nick said. "I was all right in high school. Andrew was the wild one. I was supposed to go to college."

That was surprising. Maybe it shouldn't be, but it was. "And what happened?"

"Andrew had his accident during my first semester, and I walked out and never went back. That was the end of college for me."

I stared at him. "You never told me any of this," I said. "I've done things with you that I've never done with anyone else. Never imagined doing with anyone else. And there's this whole life of yours that you never told me."

"Yeah, well, you never told me you went wild in high school after your dad died. That you stayed wild and flunked out of college. That it still affects things between you and your mom. I had to figure it out the hard way."

That was true. "This is bigger than that, though," I said. "Way bigger."

"You mad?" Nick asked.

It was a weird question, but I thought it over. "I want to punch some information out of you, but I don't think that means I'm mad. I'm hurt, though."

"Don't be," Nick said. "I don't tell anyone anything about Andrew. Not ever."

"So I'm not special," I said. "Thanks for the reminder."

He looked away from the road long enough to give me a glare, brief and molten hot. "You just met Andrew," he said. "No one meets Andrew. Don't start."

He talks about you, Andrew had said. That made my heart flip in a weird way.

"I bullied you into it," I said to him.

"No one bullies me into anything," Nick shot back.

That was sort of offensive, but it also meant that he'd taken me to meet Andrew because deep down he'd wanted to. Then I remembered. "I promised to fuck you if you did it," I said.

"And I plan to collect," Nick said, and despite everything a shiver went straight down my body, ending between my legs. There was really only one reason to go to Newcastle Point, after all. "But that isn't the only reason I did it. I think I did it because I'm sick of you not knowing. Like it matters. I don't know. With you, I don't know why I do anything anymore."

"He engineered that whole scene, didn't he?" I said. When I

looked back on it, I could see it. "Andrew, I mean. He knew before we walked in that he was going to tell me about his accident, and Lightning Man. He planned it."

"Andrew was always the smart one," Nick said. "He's scary smart. He could have left Millwood, done anything he wanted. But after the accident, he went sideways for a long time. Now it's like he's climbing the walls."

He turned at a sign that said Lookout Point, and parked. It was the off season, and there was no one else here. No teenagers in the middle of the day, no local tourists. Just us, and a view of the lake beyond us, the trees dark shadows overhead.

He turned off the car and the quiet descended. It was dark and beautiful and serene. Neither of us made a move to get out.

"Tell me," I said to Nick.

He stared ahead, seeing nothing. "It gets worse," he said.

"Well, we're here, and I'm not going anywhere," I said. "So go."

He took off his baseball cap and dropped it on the seat next to him. He ran a hand through his hair, and again I saw the two bracelets on his wrist. I was now pretty certain they had something to do with Andrew, though I didn't know what.

"He tried suicide," Nick said. "After the accident. Twice."

The silence was deafening. I felt my stomach fall, twisting as it dropped.

"Our parents checked out," Nick said, still rubbing his hand through his hair, as if that would coax the words out. "They couldn't take it after the accident. They said it was too hard. They threw money at both of us, lots of money, and never visited, never called. So there was just Andrew and me."

"Holy shit," I said softly.

He sighed. "Andrew had to go to his friend's funeral in a wheelchair. He had to adjust to being paralyzed. His whole life was fucked, his whole future. Our parents dumped us. It hit him too hard, for too long. It's like this black hole that sucks you in, and all I could do was watch. I tried to get him into therapy, on meds or something, but he's so fucking stubborn. And I couldn't be there all the time."

I was quiet. It was starting to make sense now, the deep undercurrents I'd seen between the two brothers. The history that no one else could touch. The love mixed with so many other things, like a chemical mix so unstable it can explode.

"When I was little," Nick said, "people would ask me what I wanted to be when I grew up. A baseball player, a fireman. I always said I wanted to be Andrew." He sat back in the driver's seat, leaning his head against the headrest. "I got my tattoo after his accident. It doesn't mean anything, it's just a pattern. But I felt like I should mark something that big on my skin. Make it something permanent that happened to me."

"And the bracelets?" I asked him.

He raised his hand. "This one," he said, touching the old, worn bracelet, "Andrew made for me when I was fifteen. And this one," he touched the leather one, "I put on after he tried to kill himself the first time. It's just... a reminder. That I have to be vigilant. That I can't take it off."

"Oh, Nick," I said.

He lowered his hand again. "Andrew got better, or at least better than he was. He pulled through. But I don't know if he could go back to that place. I don't know what would send him there. I'm just a guy who doesn't know a fucking thing. And I know I have to protect him against it, and I'm all he has. I almost lost him, Evie. You get it? I almost fucking lost him. Twice."

I looked at his profile. I thought of the badass guy I'd met that first night, the guy who didn't give a fuck. A guy who let everyone think he was a rich, useless waste of space. Because he couldn't let anyone see what was going on beneath the surface. Maybe that was easier for him; maybe it was the only way he could cope. "And the comics?" I said. "How do they fit in?"

"I started those when Andrew was in the hospital," Nick said. "I couldn't leave him alone, but there's only so much talking you can do, you know? So I started spinning this story about a hero called Lightning Man. He took to it right away. I'd come up with something, and he'd sketch it. He'd wake right up and almost be his old self again. So I kept it going and going. After he got home, he started redoing the artwork on his computer. I don't know how to explain it. It's just what we do."

I turned sideways in the passenger seat, drawing my knees up as I listened to him. "And if you publish it," I said, "if you publish Lightning Man, the whole process changes."

The look he shot me was so raw I nearly reached out and touched him. "If we publish it, then it isn't ours anymore," he said. "Right now it's his and mine. If it isn't his and mine anymore, then how the hell do I keep us both going?"

I did touch him then. I put my hand on his shoulder, slid it down his arm. Then I leaned in and kissed his jaw.

"Evie," he said softly.

I didn't relent. I leaned in even closer and kissed my way along the soft roughness of his short beard, to the warm place behind his ear. I kissed my way down his neck, letting my tongue taste his skin. I put my hand on his shoulder, then curled it around his neck.

He didn't push me away. He sat still, his breath coming short, and he didn't touch me. I nipped his earlobe and ran my hand down his chest to his stomach, aiming for his belt.

"Fuck," he said softly, flinching under my touch. "Fuck, fuck." He leaned over, tilted my chin, and kissed my mouth.

Immediately, I was on fire. It was the taste of him, the way he kissed me like there was no other purpose for him on earth. He pressed me back and opened my mouth and pressed into me while I ran my hands through his hair, over his back. Then down between us, tugging at his belt again.

He broke the kiss as I undid his buckle. "You want this?" he said roughly.

"Yes," I said.

He ran a thumb over my lip. "Get in the back seat," he said.

I did. I couldn't explain how exciting this was, why my whole body was on fire. It was the fact that I'd seen him, the real him, everything he'd never showed me before. It was the fact that I liked who I'd just seen, a man who took care of his brother and hated to talk about it because he cared so much. It was the fact that he was still Nick, still the guy who drove me crazy, and apparently I really wanted Nick Mason to fuck me in the back seat of his car at Newcastle Point. Something about that made me feel dirty and hot and weirdly happy.

He got in the back seat next to me and slammed the door. "Get your clothes off and get on my lap," he said.

I shivered. I was already undoing my jeans before he had all the words out of his mouth. I pushed off my shoes, my jeans, my panties, and climbed onto him, straddling him bare, I was so urgent for him. He slid his hands up under my shirt, over my nipples through my bra, then down to my ass, cupping it. In return, I tugged at his T-shirt and pulled it off.

He moved his hands up to my jaw and kissed me, our tongues tangling, my hair falling forward. It was sex and it was pure connection, as if I understood him and he understood me.

I'd kissed guys before. Made out with them. Slept with them. I'd never felt as owned as I did with Nick Mason, like I belonged to someone. Like we mattered to each other. He'd seen me fight and he'd seen me eat and he'd seen me freak out. He'd seen me drunk and he'd seen me asleep and he'd seen my ass. He'd seen me be dirty. He'd seen me come. And still here he was, cupping my face and kissing me, devouring me while his hand moved down and his fingers slid into my slick pussy, knowing every inch of the terrain.

I moved against him and we started a slow rhythm, him finger-fucking me while I moaned into his mouth. Anyone could drive by, see us, even in the dark, but I didn't care. He kissed down my neck, his beard scratching me and giving me beard burn, his fingers still moving in and out of me. I gripped his bare, muscled shoulders as my nipples went painfully hard beneath my bra.

It wasn't enough. It would never be enough until he was inside me. "Please tell me you have a condom," I said.

He laughed against my skin. It was low and sexy, that laugh, and it meant he had let everything else go, even if it was just for the moment. "Who do you think you're talking to?" he said. He squirmed beneath me, pulling out his wallet, and the next thing I heard was the condom wrapper ripping.

I unzipped his jeans and pulled them down, along with his boxers, to free his cock. "I've decided I like having a slutty boyfriend," I panted.

"You should talk, slutty girlfriend," he said, rolling the condom on. It took a moment for me to realize that we'd just admitted to being in some kind of relationship, and then he guided his cock into me and pushed my hips down.

I moaned. "Fuck, oh fuck," I panted, taking him all in. I was on top like this, in control. I lowered myself as far as I could go, feeling him go deeper and deeper inside me until we were notched together. Then I moved my hips in a slow circle.

"Fuck, like that," Nick said hoarsely, moving his hands from my hips and letting me take over. He slid them up under my shirt again instead. "Ride me nice and fucking hard."

I rocked on him, and we both groaned. He was so deep in me, making the pleasure pulse slow and hard, in my pussy and all the way inside me. I gripped his knees and he flexed his hips, moving up in rhythm with me. Slow and hard. We moved like we always did, perfectly in sync, both of us climbing to pleasure.

We were in his back seat, in public, which made it risky and dirty. Different than if we were in a bed. I used my knees to pump up and down on him and he made a different sound in his throat, moving his hand to the small of my back and splaying his fingers there. Controlling and possessive, but still letting me ride him. Which I was doing like it was the last thing I would ever do.

We hit our hard stride, chasing pleasure, unashamed, not caring about the slapping sound of our fucking, the way we were panting and saying dirty words. I just rode him as hard as I wanted, and he took it, fucking up into me and making me cry out. Sweat was starting to slicken the skin of my back under his hand, and he moved his other hand between us and rubbed his devilish, brilliant fingers over my clit just so, brushing it lightly and then more hard in an upward stroke. And I came, squeezing his hips and burying my face in his shoulder and feeling my body squeeze him over and over. And he gripped my ass and pumped up into me a few more times, hard, and I felt him come, felt every muscle of him flex against mine as his fingers dug into me.

We collapsed, me against his chest, my face still buried in his neck. I felt so good—my body on an orgasm high, my hands gripping his hot skin, his scent in my nose, his shoulder against my cheek, my cunt still pressed full of him. I was helpless against this, and I always would be. "Why is it always so good with us?" I asked against his skin.

"I don't know," he rasped, as I felt his chest rise and fall. "I'm losing my mind."

So was I. But I didn't think I minded anymore. There was no more Old Evie or New Evie, just Evie. It felt good. "What do we do now?" I asked him. Because none of this was easy.

His reply took a minute, but it was a good one. "We figure it out," he said at last. "You want to?"

My heart squeezed silently in my chest. "Yeah," I told him. "I do."

TWENTY-FOUR

One month later

Nick

Where are you right now?

The text came through on my phone, and I put down the book in my hand to read it. Evie.

In reply, I pulled up the camera and took a selfie. A wide shot that didn't just show me, but where I was: sitting on the ratty sofa in Andrew's living room, my feet up, the usual piles of junk around me. Behind my shoulder, my brother sitting at his keyboard, working away.

I didn't add any words to the message. I just hit send.

"Did you just take a picture of me, asshole?" Andrew said.

"Yeah," I replied, putting the phone down. "Deal with it."

"That's dangerous," Andrew said, clicking away. "I'm very fucking good-looking. It isn't safe to have my picture out in the world. I'm like plutonium or something."

"Evie can handle it." I picked up my book again, but put it down when another text came in. *Is that a textbook?* Evie wrote.

Of course she'd zoom in on that one thing. *Yes,* I typed back. *Studying. Test in two days.*

Tell your brother he's handsome, Evie wrote, because she knew how to butter Andrew up.

She also knew exactly how to get to me, Evie did. *Fuck off,* I wrote back. *Your turn.*

I put the phone back down while I waited. This was the new game Evie and I had been playing for weeks. When the other person asked where you were right now, you took a picture and sent it. Then the other person reciprocated. It wasn't much of a game, maybe, just a back and forth between us. I didn't even know why we kept doing it. All I knew was that I liked it when her texts came in. And I always wanted to know the answer to the question *Where are you right now?*

It would take her a second—it always took Evie a second to get up the nerve to take the picture and send it—so I picked up my book again. *Principles of Creative Writing*. Here was the fucked-up thing: I'd actually signed myself up for a creative writing course. One of those continuing education things, because come on—I needed to aim low. But so far it wasn't so bad. And I wasn't doing so bad at it. And it was the first thing I'd learned since dropping out of college five years ago. I was learning about three-act structure and character development and point of view, and fuck if it wasn't pretty interesting. The tests were about mechanics, but for the assignments I'd have to submit original work. I was thinking of a Lightning Man story already.

"Hey," Andrew said. "You think the banner should be fixed width or full width?"

"Full width," I said, flipping to the next chapter of the book.

"You don't even know what I'm talking about, do you?"

"No."

"Ugh. I'm working with amateurs here." Andrew clicked around. Outside, one of the neighbors fired up his lawn mower. It was June in the Millwood suburbs, except inside this tiny living room. In here, we had no seasons. It was fine with me.

"Despite the fact that you know nothing, I'm going with full width anyway," Andrew said. He was programming the Lightning Man website, which we were planning to launch in a few weeks. The whole thing still made me nervous, but I'd agreed to it. *If you love him, you have to do it,* Evie had told me, and she was right. So we were doing it. He was talking about apps and paid downloads and print on demand. I had no idea about any of that, though I tried to follow along.

It wasn't about the money for either of us, but the challenge and the creativity. And Andrew... Andrew was juiced. He worked on nothing except Lightning Man right now, and he had a spark that I'd never seen in him before. He fucking loved every part of this project, and he wanted me to write stories, like I always had. So maybe it would be okay to change things, like Evie said. Maybe it would work out.

I still didn't take my leather bracelet off, though. And I spent a lot of time at Andrew's when I read and studied for my course. So much time that I'd started bringing Scout with me instead of leaving her home alone. Scout was somewhere on the sofa next to me right now, where she'd burrowed beneath a pile of Andrew's laundry to sleep.

It was a pretty nice scene, all told. Except Evie wasn't here.

My phone buzzed with a text.

She'd taken the picture. The point of this game, the game where we texted the pictures, was complete honesty. You had to take the picture when the other person asked. So Evie had taken a picture of herself standing in the alleyway behind the bakery where she worked. No, the bakery where she was *manager*. She was wearing cargo pants and a V-neck T-shirt, an apron tied over her clothes, her red hair tied up loosely on the top of her head. She was holding two trash bags, and there was a dumpster behind her. *The glamorous life of a baker*, she wrote.

Even in everyday clothes, standing in front of a dumpster after going to work at four in the morning, Evie was hot. And awesome.

Take off your clothes, I texted her.

Ha, she wrote back. *You first.*

Me: *Andrew would be mad.*

Her: *So would the homeless guy sleeping in the alley right now.*

"Earth to Mason," Andrew said, pulling me out of my conversation. "You're not studying, you're staring at your redhead."

"None of your business," I told him.

He rolled his eyes. "Please. I'm ordering my own tux for the wedding. I look good in dove gray."

"Can it," I said. "We're not getting married. We're barely even dating right now."

"Which is stupid," he pointed out, "because you are."

We were dating, sort of. Evie had walked into a bakery in downtown Millwood that had advertised for a manager job, and she'd given them such a hell of an interview that they'd hired her on the spot. She supervised the bakery, managed the staff, oversaw the daily receipts, and helped with hiring and marketing. It was great, but it was also a huge learning curve, and the hours were long, at least at first. She worked a lot, and she didn't need distractions.

I was a distraction. This wasn't the kind of job she could walk into late, wearing my T-shirt after a night of nonstop sex. So I stayed away from her on work days, doing my course work and hanging with Andrew. On work days, we texted each other, but not enough to get her in trouble. On work days, I didn't even take her out to dinner, because if I did we'd end up fucking. On work days, I behaved.

On her days off, I did whatever I wanted.

Which was a lot.

On her days off, she'd come over and I'd fuck her however I wanted, as long as I wanted, as fast or slow as I wanted, until she'd come as many times as I wanted. Then we'd eat something and relax and talk about our week. Then we'd try to watch TV for about fifteen minutes, until we pulled each other's clothes off. Then we'd fuck some more. Repeat until she had to go back to work again.

Was that dating? I had no idea. It was pretty fucking great, though. So great I wanted more. But I had to be patient. Evie wasn't fucking around with her career anymore. She had her eye on owning the bakery one day, when the owner retired, and she wasn't prepared to risk that. So we didn't.

I had my own shit to take care of, anyway. I'd had to make things up with Andrew after our fight, and then we had to work out the Lightning Man details. I didn't party anymore. Instead I enrolled in my course and started studying. And coming up with more ideas. I had a thought that Lightning Man wasn't the only comic I had in me. There were at least two others buzzing around in my brain. If he was game, Andrew was going to be my comics partner for a long time.

Which was also pretty fucking great, though I didn't let myself think about it too closely.

Scout came out of her laundry burrow, blinking sleepily, and wagged her tail when she saw me. She did a wiggle, her whole hind end going back and forth, as she turned in a circle, her tongue hanging out. I patted her and she promptly rolled over, giving me her hairless belly to rub. I had to rub it with just my fingertips, because my palm was too big. She really was the stupidest dog on earth.

"What does Evie say about me?" Andrew said. "She must have said something."

"She said I'm better-looking than you."

"That's a lie. When is she coming over for dinner?"

"Never, because you can't cook."

"I'd learn."

"No. And why are you trying to impress my girlfriend?"

"Someone has to do it. You know, woo her. Give her some romance, make her feel special. And I thought she wasn't your girlfriend?"

This was classic Andrew, trying to piss me off. I was in too good a mood to fall for it. "She's my girlfriend," I said, "but she'll dump me if you cook for her, guaranteed." I closed my book, stopped rubbing Scout's belly—she jumped up immediately—and stood up. "I have to go. You need anything?"

"No, I'm good," Andrew said. "Mom brought a few things by earlier."

Right. Our mother, who had been coming to see Andrew, while avoiding me. I took how that made me feel and pushed it down, way down. "Okay then," I said.

"She'll come," Andrew said. He had turned away from his computer, turned his chair to face me. "She's just working up the nerve. But she will."

"I'm not holding my breath." I wasn't going to call her, either. If she didn't want to talk to me, there was nothing to say. I gathered my shit and my dog, said goodbye to my brother, and left.

I parked in front of my place and opened the back seat to get Scout. I tried to clip the leash to her collar, but she wasn't having it. Instead she kept standing on her hind legs, waving her front paws at me. This meant she wanted to be picked up. She was surprisingly lazy for a dog who moved almost nonstop.

I slung the gym bag from the back seat over my shoulder and picked up my textbook. Then I picked up Scout, who promptly started licking my face. "Knock it off," I told her, struggling against her small tongue while I bumped the door closed with my hip. She kept at me, aiming for the end of my nose. I hit the button to lock the car while dodging her. "Jesus, Scout, quit it."

I turned around to see a woman standing there, watching my little show. My mother.

She was about fifty now, I supposed. Still slim, her back straight, her hair dyed and styled. She wore a linen blouse and skirt that looked nice and probably cost more than Evie made in a week. She was clutching her purse and looking at me with a worried smile.

I just stood there, in my old sweatshirt, with my bag and my book and my silly dog, staring back.

"Nick," she said. "Can we talk?"

I thought I'd be cool whenever I saw her next. Instead I felt like someone had punched me in the chest and in the side of the head at the same time. "A month?" I said to her. "You've been going to see Andrew for a month, and *now* you want to talk to me?"

She winced, but she didn't turn away. "It's harder with you," she said. "You're tougher than he is. And I knew you were angry."

"You think?" I said.

"I'm sorry," Mom said, words I never thought I'd hear from her mouth. "I'm sorry about everything. And I'm sorry about what I said to you that last time, in the hospital."

I can't, Nick. I just can't. That was what she'd said when Andrew had tried to kill himself the second time. I'd called her, and she'd come, but she'd left before he woke up. *I just can't.*

I shouldn't forgive her for that. But that particular crime wasn't mine to forgive, it was Andrew's. And Andrew made his own decisions. All I wanted was to see him happy.

Scout squirmed in my arms. "I can't talk about this right now, like this," I said. We were standing in the parking lot of my building. "I have to go."

"Can we go inside and talk, then?" Mom said. "Can I come in? I have a lot of things I want to say." She paused, while I stood rigid. "Please, Nick."

Fuck. I shouldn't do it. I should tell her to just fuck off and go home, leave me to my life. I should tell her there are no second chances.

It would be easier to tell her to go. Easier not to try. Easier to just stay in my life the way it was without changing anything. To shut myself off from anyone causing me that kind of pain again. That would be the easy thing to do.

But Andrew had made me promise that if she came to me, I would listen. And I knew that Evie would agree. The easiest way wasn't always the best way in the end. We were both learning that. Sometimes you had to walk the hard route, the route that didn't have any signs. The route that could hurt you.

So I looked at my mother, at her hopeful face, and I sighed.

"All right," I said. "Come in."

TWENTY-FIVE

Two Weeks Later

Evie

Even after everything, I still liked to punch Nick Mason.

"Come on, Evie," he said. "Hit me harder."

We were at the boxing gym. We'd been here for an hour, sparring—sort of. Even though I'd upped my game, our version of sparring consisted of me hitting him, and him not hitting me back. He refused to do it any other way. *Find some other guy to hit you,* he'd told me. *I'm not fucking doing it.*

So, fine then. I hit him.

Not in the face. No way was I aiming for that gorgeous face of his. But his hot, muscled body was fair game. We dodged around the mats as I aimed for his chest, his shoulders, his stomach. He was faster than me, and I only landed some of the hits I aimed at him—and the ones I landed he ridiculed as too soft. His taunts just made me work harder, and we were both covered in sweat. My arms were shaky and my legs were rubber. I felt freaking amazing.

I positioned my feet and jabbed him again, almost getting his pec. He raised a glove and blocked me, our gloves smacking. "Better," he said. "Maybe."

I straightened, scrubbing my forearm over my sweaty forehead. "You're such an asshole," I said, panting.

"I know," Nick said. "It turns you on."

"It doesn't." It totally did.

"Right, redhead." He glanced back over his shoulder, where the gym had emptied out behind us. It was closing time, apparently. The other guys had gone and an old guy was turning out the lights.

I'd had no idea we had to go. But Nick wasn't moving. The old guy turned out a few more lights, then gave Nick a nod—which Nick returned—and walked out the front door, locking it shut behind him.

"What's going on?" I said.

"Workout's over," Nick said, his voice deceptively casual. He used his teeth to rip the velcro off his right glove.

"He just closed the place and locked us in," I pointed out.

"Yeah, he did." Nick dropped his glove and started on the other one.

We were completely alone in the place now. The lights above our mats were the only lights on. It should have been creepy or weird. Instead I watched Nick drop his other glove, and I felt a hard shiver of anticipation. He was planning something. I didn't know what it was, but I had the idea I was going to like it.

Still, I kept my voice calm, like this happened every day. "So how are we going to leave?" I asked as he stepped forward and undid my glove. "If the place is already locked, and all."

"Spare set of keys in one of the lockers in back," Nick said. "We'll lock up behind us when we go."

"Uh huh," I said. "And since we're done working out, what are we doing between now and leaving?"

"What do you think?"

The shiver of anticipation came again, harder. Oh, I liked this. He dropped my first glove and started on the other, and I just watched him. There was nothing I liked looking at more than Nick Mason. He was all muscles and scruff and bad-boy tattoos, all sweaty and mischievous and dangerous, and he was all mine. All mine.

Six weeks we'd been doing this. Playing a sort of game that was fun and hot and, underneath, deadly serious. I was managing a bakery now, working hard and long hours and loving every minute of it. I spent all day with breads and pastries and the people who loved them, and so far I was happier in my career than I'd ever been, because I'd stopped worrying about what people thought. I just went to work and came home happy, smelling like pie crust and sugar.

And on my days off, like today, I got Nick. All to myself. We played—we sparred and we talked and we took shots at each other. And the sex—oh, my god, the sex. Sometimes I thought I could spend a week locked in a room, doing nothing but having sex with Nick, and it still wouldn't be enough. We were daring and creative and sometimes wild, and the back and forth we did beforehand always added to the foreplay. With Nick, I always had to work for it. And it always paid off.

Today, he had that look in his eye, like he was going to dare me to do something. I was already wet, just looking at him and thinking about it. But there was something else going on, too. This wasn't just a sex dare. I'd done Nick's sex dares—a lot of them—and they were never quite like this.

But there was nothing I could do except wait until he was ready to show me what he was planning.

I couldn't wait.

He pulled off his shirt and mopped himself with it. I watched, appreciative. "Is this going to be a strip show?" I asked him. "I might give you a tip."

"You wish," he said, scrubbing the shirt over his face and his hair. "You know I don't strip for money. I only strip for sex."

"Is that what we're negotiating?" I said, even though I was totally already in. Still. "I'll think about it."

"You already are," said my cocky boyfriend. "You've been thinking about it for the last hour, and now you're all ready to go." He dropped the shirt and came toward me.

I crossed my arms. "I'm sweaty," I said.

"So am I," Nick said, putting his hands on my hips.

"We're in a gym," I said. "There's no way we're having sex right here, right now."

"No?" He was walking me backward. I put my hands on his biceps so I wouldn't fall, and that alone just about did me in. Nick had very nice biceps.

My butt hit something—a stack of gym mats, waist high. Oh, no. "We are not doing this," I said feebly.

His hands moved from my hips and his fingers hooked in the waist of my yoga pants. He pulled them down, along with my panties. "I've been watching your tits bounce for an hour," he said in that hot growl of his. "Five minutes and I can make you come."

"Five minutes?" My voice had definitely lost all conviction now. "Really?"

"No one's here to see." He pulled my clothes further down my thighs and pressed me back, and suddenly I was lying back on my elbows on the stack of mats while my boyfriend stripped me naked from the waist down.

I'd heard, through the grapevine, that Josh and Gina had broken up. That she'd found out he was cheating. That Josh was now with Alison, the girl from the bank with the Valentine's Day cake, and they were getting a place, moving in together. I wished her luck. I could barely remember what Josh looked like. Because apparently Nick and I were going to have sex right here, right now.

So much for revenge, then. It felt good to be free.

Nick leaned over me and kissed me. Long and hard and deep. He was hard in his shorts, and suddenly I was uncomfortable, squirming against him. Yes—five minutes was all it was going to take. I didn't care where we were anymore. I wanted that inside me, right now.

Nick slid his shorts down with one hand, ran his hand over his cock while he broke the kiss. "You ready?" he said.

"Try me," I said.

He pushed into me, and I moaned. We'd started going bare a week ago, and it made everything different all over again. There was no drug as addictive as being skin to skin with him. He must have felt the same way, because he could barely keep his hands off me, even more than usual.

But it had changed other things, too. Neither of us had ever done it bare before. It was... more intimate. More trusting. And yes, a fuck of a lot hotter.

He pressed his weight down on me, pushing in all the way, and I gripped him with my knees as he started to fuck me. "Fuck, you're hot," he growled in my ear, and I was. I was hot from watching him move for the last hour. Hot from just being around him. I moaned and pressed up into him, spreading my knees and changing the angle, and he fucked me harder. I panted as I felt the pleasure tighten inside me, start to clench my muscles. I didn't care that we were almost in public. I didn't care that we were sweaty. I just lost myself, like I always did with Nick. I let myself be dirty. I let myself love it without being embarrassed. I let everything go.

Did it take five minutes? Probably less. I only knew I came, shuddering up into him and squeezing him, my knees gripping his hips. He pushed deep into me and came too, the best feeling in the world. Then we lay there, panting.

"Okay," I said. "What was that for?"

Nick, as always, was blunt, but he stroked my temple with his thumb. "I was making you come so you'd be agreeable," he said.

"Agreeable to what?"

"Moving in to my place," Nick said. "Enough of this bullshit, Evie. Come live with me."

I stared at him. "You mean it?"

"I fucking mean it."

I couldn't breathe for a second. Live with him? Go to sleep with him every night, wake up with him every morning? Were we ready for that?

"Yes," I told him. "Yes, I'd like that."

Because he was right. We hadn't been ready for this six weeks ago. But we'd taken our time, and every day it only got better. If he was ready for this now, then so was I.

"Go home and pack a bag," he said. "Start tonight."

"Okay." I pulled him down to me and kissed him. Passionate, but sweet.

He broke the kiss and pulled off me. "Good," he said, pulling his shorts up again. "Stay there." He dug in his gym bag for a towel, which he handed to me to clean up with. I should have been embarrassed, but I wasn't.

"Is this how you always plan to convince me?" I asked when I'd pulled my yoga pants up.

"Pretty much," Nick said.

I had nothing to say to that, because it was working.

"One more thing," he said, digging into his gym bag again. "Sit back down."

I sat down on the stack of mats again, tossing the towel back into his gym bag. Because I'm classy. My chest was tight with anticipation. I didn't know he'd planned even more.

Nick came to the edge of the mats, his hips between my knees. "I'm not going to fuck you again," he told me. "You're just going to have to agree."

"Agree to what?"

"To wear this." He took my hand, turned it palm up, and put a ring in it.

A diamond ring. A slender band with a single, beautiful stone in it. The world spun for a second as I took it in. "Nick," I breathed.

"I don't want to fight with you, Evie," Nick said. "I want to marry you. When you're ready. When we're both ready. But this," he traced the ring in my palm, "this means we're gonna do it. Whenever we decide."

I closed my fingers over the ring for a second, pressing it into my palm. Then I picked it up and put it on. "I agree," I said.

He let out a breath, and I realized for the first time that he was nervous. "That's a yes?"

In answer, I leaned up and kissed him again. My arms around his neck, his around my waist, pulling me close. I felt a wave of happiness hit me harder than I'd ever imagined. He was tough and sweet and caring and funny and everything I ever wanted.

I broke the kiss, and he leaned down and kissed my jaw. "I love you," I told him.

"That's nice," he said against my neck.

I punched his arm. "Say it."

He kissed my earlobe, the tender skin beneath it. Sweet and yet very serious. "I love you, Evie Bates," he said in that sexy growl of his.

It made me shiver, so I said, "Say it again."

He was obedient for once. "I love you, Evie Bates." He kissed my neck again. "Forever. Okay?"

I thought about it. And it was perfect. It really was.

"Okay," I said to him. "Let's go shower."

ALSO BY JULIE KRISS

The Road Kings Series

Duet

Riff

The Filthy Rich Series

Filthy Rich

Sexy As Sin

Dirty Talk

Wicked Dangerous

Cold Dark Heart

The Riggs Brothers Series

Drive Me Wild

Take Me Down

Work Me Up

Make Me Beg

The Bad Billionaire Series

Bad Billionaire

Dirty Sweet Wild

Rich Dirty Dangerous

Back in Black

The Eden Hills Series

How to Date Your Brother's Best Friend

How to Date the Guy You Hate

The Mason Brothers Duet

Spite Club

Crashed

Forbidden Standalones

Forbidden

The Player

Christmas Books

My Fake Christmas Fiancé

Jingle Bell Beard

www.ingramcontent.com/pod-product-compliance
Lightning Source LLC
Chambersburg PA
CBHW032027050726
47590CB00006B/2329